22 lessons in the Art of Wizardry, plus your chance to join the Wizards' Guild

There's never been a book like this before. Real Wizardry for you to learn. The Wizard's Adventure for you to enjoy. And if you do your lessons well, you could actually be offered a place in the prestigious Wizards' Guild.

This is positively *not* fiction. This is the real thing at last. Wizardry taught by a practicing Wizard, experienced in every aspect of the art.

Just look at what you will learn . . .

- How to make a Wizard's Wand and Tools.
- How to read your future in the Wizard's Oracle.
- How to switch on Wizard's Power.
- How to build a Wizard's Castle in your mind.

Plus Star Magic, setting up a Sacred Space, and much, much more.

But that's not all. Because the *Book of Wizardry* contains the Wizard's Adventure, a magical game section that could lead you to join the Wizards' Guild and become a fully certified Wizard in your own right.

If you've ever wondered what it would be like to become a Wizard, wonder no longer. This book is for *you!*

About the Author

Cornelius Rumstuckle is a fourth generation Wizard with Old World roots. Cornelius joined the Wizards' Guild in 1514 and became its youngest-ever president seventy-eight years later, a post he holds to this day.

To Write to the Author

If you wish to contact the author or would like more information about this book, please write to the author in care of Llewellyn Worldwide and we will forward your request. Both the author and publisher appreciate hearing from you and learning of your enjoyment of this book and how it has helped you. Llewellyn Worldwide cannot guarantee that every letter written to the author can be answered, but all will be forwarded. Please write to:

Cornelius Rumstuckle
℅ Llewellyn Worldwide
P.O. Box 64383, Dept. 0-7387-0165-3
St. Paul, MN 55164-0383, U.S.A.

Please enclose a self-addressed stamped envelope for reply,
or $1.00 to cover costs. If outside U.S.A., enclose
international postal reply coupon.

Many of Llewellyn's authors have websites with additional information and resources. For more information, please visit our website at
http://www.llewellyn.com

CORNELIUS RUMSTUCKLE

The BOOK OF WIZARDRY

THE APPRENTICE'S GUIDE TO THE SECRETS OF THE WIZARDS' GUILD

2003
Llewellyn Publications
St. Paul, Minnesota 55164-0383, U.S.A.

First Edition
Third Printing, 2003

Book design by Donna Burch
Cover art and interior illustrations © 2002 by Eric Hotz
Cover design by Kevin R. Brown

Library of Congress Cataloging-in-Publication Data

Rumstuckle, Cornelius, 1940–
    The book of wizardry : the apprentice's guide to the secrets of the wizard's guild / Cornelius Rumstuckle.— 1st ed.
        p.   cm.
    Summary: Gives the twenty-two secrets for becoming a Wizard, including how to make a wand, read an oracle, and achieve member status in the Wizards' Guild.
    ISBN 0-7387-0165-3
        1. Magic—juvenile literature. [1. Magic. 2. Wizards.] I. Title.

BF1611.R85 2003
133.4'3—dc21   2003044691

Llewellyn Publications
A Division of Llewellyn Worldwide, Ltd.
P.O. Box 64383, Dept. 0-7387-0165-3
St. Paul, MN 55164-0383, U.S.A.
www.llewellyn.com

Contents

So, You Want
to Be a Wizard . . .

It's not easy, you know. Not easy at all. Some people spend their whole lives trying to work magic and never really get the hang of it, poor things.

Of course you'll have this book to help you.

That's never happened before, not in the whole history of Wizardry. There has never been an official handbook of the Wizards' Guild issued to just anyone.

I'm not sure I approve.

But still, they've given me the job of teaching you, so that's what I'm going to do. By the time you've worked your way through this book, you'll be a Wizard all right. And a good one, even if it kills me.

Maybe you'll even be good enough to join the Wizards' Guild.

That's a long way down the road, of course. You'll have to work your way right through this book before you even think about it. And I mean *work*. No goofing off the way you do at school.

If you're serious about becoming a Wizard, you'll need to start at the beginning and work your way right through to the end. You'd think that would be obvious, but I've known some who tried it backwards. I've even known a few who started at the middle and worked in both directions at once. You won't hear much more of them, I can tell you.

Here's how it will happen.

First, I'll teach you the Theory of Wizardry. Don't imagine you can skip that part, because you can't. I'm not having the country full of Wizards who don't know what they're doing. Far too dangerous.

Besides, you'll need a bit of theory if you're going to survive the Wizard's Adventure.

You're not to start the work until you understand the theory. Not a wand will you make, not a spell will you cast until you know exactly what you're doing. I won't have it. So study the theory carefully. (It's not all that hard.) Then, when you've got the hang of it, you can go on to your next lesson.

That's what they are—lessons. And lessons mean work. Work, work, work. It's no good just reading about something. You have to *do* it. You have to try it out. Nobody ever got to be a Wizard just by reading a book and snapping their fingers.

Some of the work is making things, like wands or talismans to bring you luck. Some of it is making something of yourself. Changing the way you think. Learning how to use your mind. That sort of thing. What goes on inside a Wizard's head is a lot different than what goes on inside anybody else's.

The lessons are graded. When you get through the first seven—and that means doing all the work—you can call yourself a Trainee Wizard in the First Degree. If you manage the next five, you become a Trainee Wizard in the Second Degree. Complete the six after that and you have my permission to give yourself the Third Degree.

If you want to go further than that, you'll have to do a few advanced lessons and survive the Wizard's Adventure.

The Wizard's Adventure looks like a game. It plays like a game. It's fun like a game. But it *isn't* a game. It's a cunningly disguised examination. It's an examination with a spell cast on it so it seems like a game. You can do things like that when you've practiced Wizardry as long as I have.

You'll need dice, pen and paper, and a pendulum for the Wizard's Adventure, so make sure you have them ready when the time comes. Don't worry about the pendulum right now. By the time you reach the Wizard's Adventure, I'll

have told you how to make a pendulum and, more importantly, how to use it. So make sure to do every lesson in the book. Because you won't get through the Adventure if you don't.

But if you do get through the Wizard's Adventure, you'll learn the secret of the Wizards' Guild. The one that lets you join. When you do, you're not a Trainee any more. You're a fully accredited Wizard. You'll get your Wizarding Certificate and your Wizard's Code.

Have I forgotten anything?

Yes, I have. You're going to keep a journal. The Wizards' Guild doesn't hold with sloppy magic. So everything has to be neat and tidy. That way, if anything goes wrong, we know who to blame afterward. Get yourself a notebook, and don't use it for anything else. It doesn't have to be fancy, but you can decorate it a bit, if you like.

Have I forgotten anything else?

If I have, that's just too bad. Now you'll learn the Theory of Wizardry, so pay attention.

Pay *very close* attention.

Lesson One:
The Theory of Wizardry

Wizardry works from the inside out.

There, I've said it. That's one of the biggest Wizard secrets there is. Used to be they'd lock you in a crystal cave for telling anybody that one. Or burn you at the stake. But there you have it, right up front for everyone to see.

Wizardry works from the inside out.

Bet you don't know what it means, though. I feel funny coming right out and explaining, but that's what I'm going to do. Here goes . . .

If you want to work magic—real magic, not conjuring or any other sort of tricks—you have to look inside your head. Even when you're using things like wands or spells or secret symbols, the magic starts between your ears.

Try it now. Sit down, close your eyes, and find out what's in your head.

Dark, isn't it?

And noisy. You keep chattering to yourself. Yes, you do. All the time. Every minute of your waking day it's talk, talk, talk, talk, chitter, chatter, chatter. We'll have to do something about that later, but first I want you to do something about the dark. I want you to imagine a bright light.

Now notice a couple of things.

The first is that it isn't dark inside your head anymore. You've made it light. You've redecorated the inside of your head.

The second is that you have control of what goes on in there. You just switched on a light. You can switch it off again as easily. Inside your head, you can do anything you want. That's what I mean by control.

Let's try using a bit of that control now. Instead of just imagining a bright light, I want you to imagine a country scene: woods, hills, grass, a stream, happy cows—all that nonsense.

Not difficult, was it? Not difficult at all. Even though there's a lot more to imagine in a country scene than there is in a bright light, you did it just as easily. I expect that's because you've already had a lot of practice daydreaming.

(Oh, yes, I know all about your daydreaming, too. And I know the sort of things you daydream about. Disgraceful. Quite disgraceful.)

But let me tell you what you're doing now isn't *just* daydreaming. It's controlled daydreaming and there's a huge difference. Here comes the next big secret of Wizardry:

If you take control of what goes on inside your head, you take control of what goes on outside it.

Sounds really easy, doesn't it? Makes you wonder why everybody isn't a Wizard, doesn't it? Well, it's not easy! Just try this:

Get a watch to time yourself, then stop thinking. See how long you can go without a single thought.

Ha-ha! What did you manage? Twenty minutes? Ten? Five? Not even a minute? You're very lucky if you can even go ten seconds without thinking, unless you've trained yourself. You sit there with your mind a blank, then you think "Hey, I'm not thinking!" Splat! You just started thinking again.

Which brings me to the final secret of Wizardry:

You get control of what's inside your head the same way you get to Carnegie Hall.

You know how you get to Carnegie Hall? Of course you do—practice! You'll have lots of opportunities to practice stuff inside your head while you're training as a Wizard.

Okay, that's enough theory for the minute. Let's get to something more exciting. Do the task that's set for this lesson—it'll take you all of about eight seconds. I believe in breaking in young Wizards gradually—then I'll tell you how to find your secret Wizard Name.

TASK FOR LESSON ONE

Write the three secrets of Wizardry into your Wizard's Journal, then see if you can fly a broomstick. (Just kidding about the broomstick.)

Lesson Two:
The Secret Name

Every Wizard has a secret name.

Not many people know that, because Wizards are good at keeping secrets. It's true all the same. When you meet a Wizard, he'll only ever introduce himself by his outer name, never his secret name. Even when two Wizards know each other, they never—ever—tell each other their secret names.

There's a very good reason. Anybody who knows your secret name has a special power over you. You'll see why in a minute.

Before I tell you how to find your secret name, I want to tell you something very, very important. Nobody can find your secret name for you. You have to find it for yourself.

You need to know that because there are people around who claim they have the power to give you your secret name. Or sell you your secret name as if it were a pound of

butter. If you ever meet people like that, give them a mysterious smile and go on your way.

Here's how to find your secret name.

First, know you can take as much time as you need to do
this. In fact, know that you *should* take as much time as you
need to do this. The Quest for Your Secret Name can take
just a few minutes, but it can just as easily take weeks or
months. Don't get hung up about the time. Discovering your
secret name is one of the most important bits of Wizardry
you will ever undertake. So treat it seriously and take as much
time as you need.

Now sit in your room or take a walk on the beach or
whatever you do when you want to be alone . . . and do
some heavy thinking about yourself.

Try to find out who and what you really are. Try to figure what you really want to do. See if you can dig down deep
inside yourself until you find the core, the one thing that expresses your deepest belief, your strongest insight about
yourself or the world. Find the words that most clearly de-
scribe what makes you—*you!*

Be honest with yourself. You're not going to tell anybody
what you find: not your mother, your father, your sisters,
your brothers, your teachers, or your friends. You're not
going to tell me or any of your fellow Wizards. So there's absolutely nobody for you to impress and nothing you need
feel ashamed about. You are who you are and that's what
you're trying to find.

When you get to that deep hidden core that best expresses
who you are, create a motto. If you're happy with what you

found, you can have the motto express it. If you aren't, then the motto should express your determination about what you hope to become.

For example, if you find you're the sort of person who values honesty above everything else, you might have a motto that says *Honesty Is My Life.* Then again, you might discover you're a shy sort—many Wizards are. Since it seems a bit silly to have a motto like *The Meek Shall Inherit the Earth If That's All Right with Everybody Else,* you might like to turn it into an aspiration: *Courage Will Be My Companion* or something of that sort.

Here are a few secret mottoes of real Wizards. (They're all dead now, so I can tell them to you.)

Royal Is My Race
With God As My Shield
I Shall Endure

Nice ring to them, isn't there? See if you can create a motto with that sort of noble feel. But here's the thing. Never, never tell anybody—and I mean *anybody*—your motto, because your motto is your secret name. Don't even write it down. If you have to write something down, just write the initials. RIMR (Royal Is My Race). WGAMS (With God As My Shield). Better still, translate the motto into another language and write down the initials of that.

For example, if you're a sort of Napoleon character and you've decided the motto that best expresses who you are is *I'll Beat the Lot of You,* your motto initials don't have to be

IBTLOY. You could translate it into Latin—*Omnia Vinces*, "I will overcome everything"—and just have the initials OV.

Got the hang of it? Good. Now off you go and discover your secret name.

TASK FOR LESSON TWO

Write the *initials* of your secret name in your Wizard's Journal.

Lesson Three:
The Wizard's Cup

Now I'd better tell you about the Five Elements.

The Five Elements have nothing to do with the chemical elements you learn about at school. And they've nothing to do with the elements that get you wet and miserable when you go out in them. The Five Elements are just the way we Wizards divide the world up for our own convenience. The Five Elements are:

Earth
Air
Fire
Water
And the one that tops them all—Spirit.

Think of them as boxes you put things in. Anything at all. Let's say you had a fever. Would you put the fever under Earth, Air, Fire, or Water? Fire, of course. It's hot. You're burning up. Fever has to be classified under the Element Fire. How about a tornado? That's Air—Air at its worst, but definitely Air. A slab of rock has to be Earth. The Atlantic Ocean? Couldn't be anything else but Water.

Now you try. What Element is soil? What Element is a river? What Element is breath? What element is a volcanic eruption? Easy peasy—Earth . . . Water . . . Air . . . Fire. No problem at all. You can file anything under its Elemental label. You can even file mythic creatures. (At least we're going to pretend they're mythic. Wizards know they're not mythic at all, although you don't see them around our world much these days.) Here are some "mythic" creatures:

Gnomes—Earth
Sylphs—Air
Salamanders—Fire
Undines—Water

You can file directions under their Elemental labels. Like this:

East—Air
South—Fire
West—Water
North—Earth

You can file seasons under their Elemental labels:

Spring—Air
Summer—Fire
Fall—Water
Winter—Earth

You can file—wait a minute. You want to make a wand? Of course you want to make a wand. Every Wizard wants to make a wand. You can make a wand in a minute, after I've finished with the Elements. And I'm just coming to the important bit. The important bit is this. You can file magical tools under their Elemental labels:

Wing—Air
Wand—Fire
Cup—Water
Disk—Earth

You're going to make all those Elemental Tools, including the Wand. You're going to start with the Cup. I know you want me to start with the Wand, but you're going to start with the easiest and work your way up to the hardest. It's for your own good, so stop complaining.

The Cup

The Cup is associated with Water because cups hold liquids. Here's how you make it:

First you take some molten glass and blow it into the shape of a cup.

Gotcha!

Mind you, there was a time when that's what you would have had to do. Read the really old Wizard's books and they all told you to make everything from scratch. You wanted a magic sword, you had to dig iron ore out of the ground and smelt it. Then beat out the blade in a forge. Then forge the handle. If you wanted leather for the grip, you had to skin a cow. Dreadful waste of time. Fortunately nowadays you can use ready-made items.

You're going to have to get yourself something that will work as a cup. Nothing with a handle on it. You want a beaker or a goblet, or you can use a glass. It can be made out of glass, or ceramic, or wood, or metal (pewter is good) or anything you like, really. But *try* to avoid plastic. I know some modern Wizards swear by plastic, but in my experience it doesn't work as well, although you can use it if you're really, really desperate.

Your parents may have something suitable they'd give you. *Don't borrow it without telling them*. You're going to turn this cup into a magical tool so you can't give it back. If there's nothing you can find around the house, you're just going to have to earn the money to *buy* your cup. Search your local supermarket or try a garage sale. Given time, you'll find something you can afford.

When you have your cup, you have to turn it into a Magic Cup. There are two ways you can do that.

The first is to wash it thoroughly under cold running water, then leave it out under a full moon overnight. The cup will absorb the moon's rays and take on what Wizards call a *charge*. Bring it in early next morning and wrap it in a clean white cloth until you need to use it.

The thing about charging by moonlight is you have to wait for a *full* moon, which might be a month away when you read this, and you have to wait for a clear night, which might take even longer. So you might want a faster way to do the job, in which case you'll find this second method works just as well:

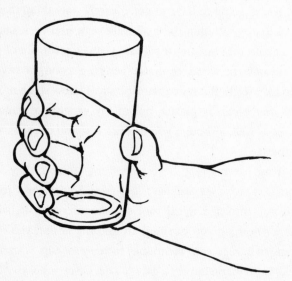

Once again wash your Cup thoroughly under cold running water. Find somewhere you won't be disturbed. Sit down comfortably and hold the Cup in both hands on your lap. Close your eyes and chant:

> *Wizard's Cup. Wizard's Cup.*
> *Filling up. Filling up.*
> *Magic might, shining bright*
> *Fill the Cup with sparkling light!*

As you chant, imagine a bright blue moonbeam coming down from heaven to fill the Cup with sparkling light.

When you open your eyes, the Cup will be charged and ready for use. Here again, wrap it up in a clean, white cloth until you need it.

Okay, this lesson has gone on quite long enough. Here's your task, although I expect you've guessed what it is already.

TASK FOR LESSON THREE
Make the Wizard's Cup.

Lesson Four:
The Wizard's Wing

After the Cup, the next easiest thing to make is the Wizard's Wing.

You remember how each of the Wizard's Tools was associated with an Element? The Cup you made was associated with Water. The Wizard's Wing is associated with Air.

You'll need seven feathers for your Wizard's Wing. They all have to be roughly the same size, and the feathered blade part should be no more than a foot long. But the most important thing about these feathers is that they should be a gift to you from the birds that grew them. That means you have to find them. You have to find them on the ground. You can't buy them. You can't take them. It's no use sneaking off to pluck a chicken. You have to *find* them.

Now here's another Wizard's secret. *The things you really need will come to you.*

If you really need those feathers, if you're really serious about making your Wizard's Wing, then the feathers will turn up. Just keep your eyes open. Bird fly all over the planet and they're forever dropping feathers. Look in your garden. Look under trees. Have patience and they'll come to you. Maybe one at a time, maybe all together, but they'll come.

Don't worry about the type of feather or the color. If you live near the sea, you're most likely to find white feathers from a gull. If you don't, you could just as easily find black feathers from a crow. Either is fine, or a mixture of the two, or some other feather altogether. You could be reading this book up the Amazon river, for all I know, in which case the world might present you with bright red feathers from a parrot. They're all good. So long as you find them, they'll help you work your magic.

You may not find them all at once, but that's okay. Keep your eyes open, have patience, and eventually you'll have all seven. And those seven gifted feathers will make up the blade of your Wizard's Wing. Here's how:

Place the feathers together so they lie flat against one another. They'll probably be different sizes, but that's all right. Just forget about size and lay them together so the quills at the end all line up. You should have enough of the quills exposed so you can grip the bunch of feathers comfortably in one hand. If any quill isn't naturally long enough, you can pick off bits of feather until it is.

Now get a length of the strongest, bright yellow ribbon you can find, and wrap it carefully around the quills to create a handle. Make sure the ribbon covers the quills completely.

This binding with the ribbon not only keeps the Wing together and forms a handle, but gives it the color yellow associated with the Air element.

Nearly there.

To charge your Wing ready for use, wait for a breezy day. Slip outside somewhere quiet where you won't be disturbed, hold the Wing by its handle above your head, close your eyes, and chant:

> *Wizard's Wing. Wizard's Wing*
> *Power of Air. Power of Air.*
> *Call the magic as I sing*
> *To charge all seven feathers fair!*

As you chant, imagine a bright yellow sunbeam coming down from heaven to bathe the Wing in its light. When you open your eyes, the Wing will be charged and ready for use. Wrap it in a clean, white cloth until you need it.

TASK FOR LESSON FOUR
Make your Wizard's Wing.

Lesson Five:
The Wizard's Disk

Most people don't know what a Wizard's Disk is. That's good. The less they know, the better. The important thing is that *you* know what a Wizard's Disk is.

A Wizard's Disk (sometimes called a pentacle or pantacle, and not to be confused with a pentagram, which is something else entirely) is a wooden disk with a special design on it, associated with the Element Earth. There's nothing really like it outside of Wizardry.

It's not hard to make, especially if you're any good at painting. Since blank wooden disks of the right size are very hard to find, you can use cardboard instead. Draw a circle 2½ inches in diameter on a piece of plain, stiff cardboard, and cut your disk out carefully using a pair of scissors.

First, get together your paints. Watercolors aren't much good, so try to find poster paints, acrylic, or oil paints. Best of all is good quality gloss paint. You won't need very much, but you will need different colors, so make sure you have:

Black
White
Pale Yellow (Citrine)
Reddish Brown (Russet)
Army Green (Olive)

If you're having trouble deciding on the citrine, olive, or russet colors, ask an adult for help.

To make your Wizard's Disk, just copy this diagram on both sides of your cardboard cut-out. If you find that a little tricky, you can trace over the diagram in this book (it's the right size for a 2½-inch disk), cut out your tracing, and glue it onto your cardboard Disk. Repeat the process for the back, then carefully paint the colors in the right places.

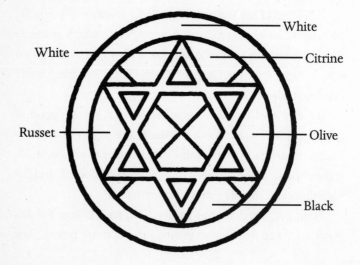

When your Disk is finished, and the paint has completely dried, wrap it carefully in something waterproof, like a plastic bag, and bury it in soil (a window box will do if you haven't a garden) for a day and a night. Immediately after you've buried it, close your eyes and chant:

Wizard's Disk. Wizard's Disk.
Solid, sturdy power of Earth
Touch the tool that I have made
And bring it to a magic birth!

As you chant, imagine the rich, brown energies of Earth soaking like dark syrup through the waterproof wrapping to bring your Disk alive. When you dig up your Disk after a day and a night, it will be charged ready for use. Throw away the waterproof wrapping and wrap the Disk itself in a clean, white cloth until you need it.

TASK FOR LESSON FIVE
You've guessed it—make the Disk.

Lesson Six:
The Wizard's Wand

You're not much of a Wizard if you haven't got a Wand. But you can forget those things you see in movies, with all the tinsel. Wands come in different shapes and sizes, but no tinsel.

You can also make them out of different things. Oddest Wand I ever saw was made from steel. My friend the Wizard Mim had it given to him in Malaysia. Plain shaft with a metal hoop at one end. When you spin it, a phantom Wand appears inside the hoop. Very spooky.

My own Wand's made from crystal, bladed, with a golden handle and a polished rock crystal ball on top. Sort of a cross between a Wand and a knife. Given to me by my love, of course. There are only two ways you can get a decent Wand. One is to have it given to you. The other is to make it for yourself. If you buy yourself a Wand—and there are lots for sale—it never seems to work right.

The Wand I'm going to teach you how to make in this lesson is a Fire Wand. You'll probably need some other Wands when you get into Advanced Wizardry, but a Fire Wand is the Wand to start with. An admirable Wand. Looks good, not so big you'll have trouble hiding it from prying eyes, nice balance in the hand.

Here's how you make it:

First, you need a plain wooden rod no more than 18 inches long. My Fire Wand is actually a lot shorter—18 inches is the absolute maximum—so you can make something that feels comfortable for the size of your hand. A piece of bamboo will do—pick one three segments long; you'll find out why in a minute—or you can even use some tightly rolled and glued construction paper.

Paint the whole thing flame red, with a nice strong gloss paint. Really bright scarlet—what the British call pillar-box red. When it's dry, divide the rod up into three segments by painting on two sets of two bright yellow bands. If you're using bamboo, the bands will coincide with the knots so they'll be raised a bit.

Now on the last two inches at one end of your Wand, paint wavy stripes, again in bright yellow, so they look like flames. You can tip the flames with a spot of orange if you like, but that's not compulsory.

When you've finished, and the paint is completely dry, you should then charge your Fire Wand as follows:

Wait until the sun is shining, then go outside somewhere you won't be disturbed. Raise your Fire Wand so the end with the painted flames points into the sun (but don't *look* into the sun—that'll make you blind), then close your eyes and chant:

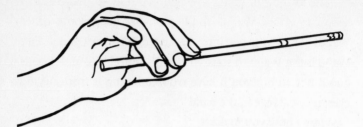

Wizard's Wand. Wizard's Wand.
Power of Fire and power of flame
Flow into this mighty rod
So I may have a Wizard's fame!

As you chant, imagine giant flames leaping from the sun to be sucked into the structure of your Wand. When you open your eyes, your Wand will be charged ready for use. Wrap it in a clean, white cloth until you need it.

Here's the task for this lesson:

TASK FOR LESSON SIX
Now, at last, you get to do it. Take a deep, deep breath and make your very own Fire Wand!

Lesson Seven:
Using the Wizard's Tools

Now you've made your Wizard's Tools, what are you going to do with them?

Not very much, if I have my way. Wizard's Tools are for advanced magic, not the trainee stuff. I'm not even going to tell you how to *dedicate* your Wizard's Tools until you join the Wizards' Guild. That way you won't even be tempted to do anything silly.

But since you've taken the trouble of making them and charging them, this little lesson will give you some very useful hints about how you might use them later on, as well as an interesting experiment you can try right now.

I've already told you that the four Elements of Earth, Air, Fire, and Water are boxes you can put things into. Now I want to tell you that they're also *energies*. That's to say, each one is a particular type of energy—earthy energy, airy energy, fiery energy, watery energy.

In their very purest form, these energies really only exist inside your head. I'll be talking to you a lot more about all this later, but for now just take my word for it that the purest form of the various elemental energies exists in the world of your imagination.

What the Wizard's Tools do is help you bring those energies through from the world of your imagination to the ordinary physical world around you. Each Tool acts as a channel for its own special energy. The Disk conducts Earth energy from inside your head to the outside world. The Wizard's Wing conducts Air energy. The Wand conducts Fire energy. The Cup conducts Water energy. All these energies start inside your head, but emerge into the physical world through your Wizard's Tools.

I know that sounds spooky, but then a lot of Wizardry is spooky.

Now the thing is, you don't want to dump a whole lot of spooky energy into the world and just let it run around upsetting people. No, you don't—just behave yourself. Any energy you bring through needs to be controlled. It needs to have a purpose.

Actually, bringing raw energy through from the inside of your head and dumping it into the physical world doesn't really do very much. It's a bit like electricity. Very useful stuff, electricity, but if you don't have your house wired, it won't do a thing for you except produce the occasional thunderstorm.

Generally speaking, Wizards control elemental energies using rituals. A ritual is the equivalent of wiring your house, but it's a complicated process and one I don't want to get into here in any detail. Let me just say that an important part of any elemental ritual is the Wizard's Tools. They help you bring the energies through and the ritual directs them into something useful.

As I'm not going to go any further into ritual here—it's far too advanced for you yet—I will give you just the tiniest taste of what it feels like to bring through a little elemental energy using a Wizard's Tool. Here's what I want you to do:

First, make a picture of the Earth Element inside your head. You can do this by imagining soil, or country scenes, plants growing—all that sort of thing. While you're making the pictures, try to sense the *essence* of the scenes, their earthiness, the thing that makes you think of Earth when you look at them.

Once you've caught this essence, take up your Earth Disk and hold it in both hands. Let the essence of Earth flow out of your mind into the Disk, then out from the Disk into your body.

Once you get the hang of this, your body will begin to feel very strong, very solid, but also very heavy and cumbersome. Don't worry about this; it's just a sign you're doing it right and the rest of the exercise will balance everything out again.

Next, make a picture of the Air Element inside your head. Imagine the sky, imagine clouds, imagine wind and storms. Once again, try to sense the essence that makes you think Air when you imagine them. Now take up your Wizard's Wing, hold it in both hands, let the essence of Air flow out of your mind into the Wing, then out from the Wing into your body.

As the energy of the Air Element enters your body, you'll feel it counteracting the heaviness that came with the Earth Element. You'll still feel stronger, but now your strength is easier to carry. You'll feel lighter, able to move more easily.

See what you're doing? You're introducing elemental energies into your body to stimulate the elemental energies already there.

When you get to know yourself really well,* you can top up any elemental energy that's running low, but for now it's best to bring in these energies in a balanced way. So now, having brought in Earth and Air, you should begin to imagine infernos, hearth fires, forest fires, rolling billows of flame.

Now take your Fire Wand in both hands, catch the essence of Fire in your mental pictures, and let it flow into the Wand, then flow out again into your body. You will feel an immediate surge of raw energy (and may even start to feel quite hot), which can be very striking.

Finally, balance off the Fire—before it gets too hot—by making mental pictures of pools, rain, seas, oceans. Take up your Wizard's Cup in both hands, direct the watery essence of your mental pictures into the Cup, then let it flow outward into your body. As you do so, the Fire energy will gather itself into a pleasant furnace in the pit of your stomach, while the Water essence will produce a sensation of flexibility so you can tackle even difficult tasks more easily and imaginatively than you've done before.

It'll also prepare you for some interesting Wizardry you'll learn at a later date.

---

* Which you'll need to do if you're ever going to practice Wizardry really well.

TASK FOR LESSON SEVEN

Bring through the four elemental energies as described in this lesson, then wrap up each Wizard's Tool carefully in a piece of clean white cloth, and put them all away somewhere your little sister won't find them. Never show off your Wizard's Tools to anybody and never ever let anyone else handle them except you.

Have you completed the tasks for the first seven lessons? No cheating, mind you. No pretending you've made a Fire Wand if you haven't.

If you've read the lessons and completed all seven tasks, pat yourself on the back—use a back scratcher if your arm won't reach—mysteriously smile, and have yourself a little celebration. You've just become . . .

Trainee Wizard
in the First Degree
is Honorarily Conferred Upon

_____

Name

This _____ day of _____

in the year _____

As Recognition of Distinction
in being a Wizard's Apprentice
with license to practice his
or her trade & mystery

Cornelius Rumstuckle

_____

Cornelius Rumstuckle
Wizard Grand Master

Lesson Eight:
The Wizard's Oracle

Think you'll make Trainee Wizard in the Second Degree? Well, let's find out. One of the great things about being a Wizard is you get to look into the future. Or at least you get to try.

Divination, which is what Wizards call predicting the future, has a long and honorable history. Right back in pre-historic times, hairy great Cave-Wizards were figuring ways to discover whether they would end up as a saber-tooth tiger's lunch.

Some of the early methods were pretty gross. In Roman times, they cut up chickens and read the future from their guts. (Don't ask.) Some were pretty dangerous. In ancient Greece they breathed in volcanic fumes until they fell down raving. Some were just plain tricky, like seeing visions in a polished piece of rock crystal.

I'm going to teach you two methods of divination, neither of which involves dead animals, volcanoes, or lumps of
polished rock. The first you can use anywhere, at any time,
without equipment. The second's a bit more complicated
and needs some special equipment that you're going to have
to make.

Okay, here's the first. It's called the Pyramid Oracle and
it's based on mathematics.

Come back! Come back here at once! You're training to
be a Wizard now. You can't let a little thing like mathematics
frighten you. Besides, it's *simple* mathematics. Just sums really.
Sort of thing you learned when you were six. If you can add,
you can do this divination.

First, what do you want to find out about? Think of the
question you want to ask and ask it *in your own words*. I can't
begin to tell you how important that bit is. It has to be in
your own words. When you've figured out your question
and how to ask it, write it down.

Let's assume your question was *Will I make it as a Wizard*?
You probably wouldn't have put it that way. You probably
would have asked something like *O mighty mathematical magic,
shall I become the greatest Wizard of the Twenty-First Century*? But
for the sake of the example, we'll keep it to *Will I make it as a
Wizard*?

What you do now is count the number of letters in each
word of your question and write them down in a row, one
after the other. (This means, incidentally, that you can ask the
question in any language in the world and the method still

works. Neat, eh?) So for *Will I make it as a Wizard?* you would write down:

$$4\ 1\ 4\ 2\ 2\ 1\ 6$$

Will = 4 . . . *I* = 1 . . . *make* = 4 . . . *it* = 2 . . . *as* = 2 . . . *a* = 1 . . . *Wizard* = 6 (you don't count the question mark). As it happens, every word in my example added up to a single-digit number, less than 10. If you use very long words that add up to 10 or more, you *reduce* these to a single number by adding together the digits. So 10 would be 1+ 0, which equals 1; 11 would be 1 + 1, which equals 2; 12 would be 1 + 2, which equals 3, and so on. If you happen to use a word like *antidisestablishmentarianism,** which is the longest word in the English language and has 28 letters in it, then 2 + 8 = 10, which still isn't a single-digit figure, so you have to add the digits again—1 + 0 = 1.

Now break the numbers you've written down into pairs, like this: (4 and 1) (4 and 2) (2 and 1). Since 6 hasn't another number to pair with, you leave it on its own.

Following this so far? Good. Add each pair of numbers together and write down the result. In my example, it comes to 4 + 1 = 5, 4 + 2 = 6, 2 + 1 = 3, and 6 + 0 = 6. So you write down:

$$5\ 6\ 3\ 6$$

Now do it again, breaking your new numbers into pairs and adding them together. So (5 and 6) (3 and 6) . . . but when you go to add the first two together, there's a small

---

* Well, you might. You might ask, "Is antidisestablishmentarianism ever likely to become a political issue in the State of Georgia?" It would be a fairly dumb question, but you might ask it.

problem. You only work with single numbers in this system and $6 + 5 = 11$. So once again you add together the *digits* of the number you got: $1 + 1 = 2$.

When you go through adding the pairs of numbers in the last line, you have $6 + 5 = 11$, which reduces $1 + 1 = 2$; and then you have $3 + 6 = 9$. So your next number is:

2 9

I expect you know what you're going to do now. That's right, add $2 + 9$. Since this makes 11, you add the two digits together $(1 + 1)$ and end up with:

2

What you've actually done is create a sort of number pyramid* with your original number at the bottom. Look:

2

2 9

5 6 3 6

4 1 4 2 2 1 6

From now on when you use this method, write the numbers like that, each result going above the line before. What you're looking for every time is that number at the top of the pyramid—2 in my example. Once you have the top number, you have the answer to your question. Because each number from 1 to 9 has its own meaning. Just read the answer from the table following:

1 Yes. Yes, yes, yes! Definitely, categorically yes.
Success. Absolutely. No doubt about it.

---

* Which is why it's called the Pyramid Oracle, duh!

2   No. You're not going to win this one. Failure. Bummer. Try something else. (Or at least try some other way.)

3   Yes, but only if you try really hard. Mind you, there could be an unexpected bonus from this when you do succeed.

4   Probably not. You're more likely to fail than succeed if you go for this now. There's something you need that just isn't here yet. You can risk it if you like, but maybe better to try again at some other time.

5   This should come out okay eventually, but you will have to exercise patience. When it does come out okay, you'll gain by it.

6   Conditions are favorable, but you'll have to use your head. If you don't, this one could still fail.

7   This *should* come out all right, but only if you lay the foundations carefully and there aren't too many people hassling you about what you're up to. Otherwise . . . well, it probably won't be a disaster, but it won't be up to much either.

8   It's very likely to go down the tubes because you're not putting in the effort that's needed. Either that or you're going to be let down by others involved. You might just turn this one around if you use really good judgment.

9   You'll succeed, but only after a struggle. And, to tell you the truth, it might not turn out the way you expect either.

So the answer to my question *Will I make it as a Wizard?* is **2** which means—wait a minute, that can't be right! Of course I'll make it as a Wizard. I've *already* made it as a—*Hrumph!* Well, it was only an example question anyway. I mean I wasn't *really* asking the Oracle about my future.

I think I'll go on to the next one now.

The trouble with the Pyramid Oracle (apart from the fact it gives stupid answers to example questions) is that you can only use it for simple queries. Sometimes you need a fuller answer. That's where the second oracle comes in. I call this one the Wizard's Oracle. Actually you might even call it the Welsh Wizard's Oracle since, as far as I can discover, it was invented in Wales. To work it, you'll need three dice and a special bit of equipment.

The special bit of equipment looks like this:

This circle is about 2 to 2½ feet in diameter. You can draw it on a large sheet of paper or cardboard.

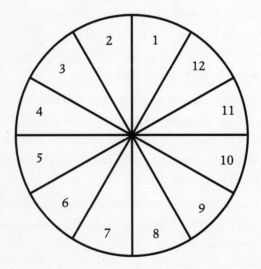

If you'll take my advice, you'll paint it, in white, on a large piece of black cloth—that way you'll have something that's easy to take with you anywhere. Mark it out first lightly in chalk. You can draw the outer circle using a thumb-tack and a piece of thread. Put your cloth on a wooden board, press in the thumbtack where you want the middle of the circle. Now tie a piece of thread around 1 to 1¼ feet long to the tack at one end and the chalk at the other. Once you've done that, you can draw a perfect circle easily.

Using a ruler, divide the circle up as shown. Make a right-angled cross first, then draw in the other divisions by eye. Number them counterclockwise (one of the few times a Wizard works counterclockwise) then, if you're satisfied with the result, paint over the chalk guidelines to make the whole thing permanent.

You can use this Oracle to answer your own questions or those of friends. Here's how:

First ask your question.

Actually that isn't as stupid as it sounds. Lots of people are really fuzzy about the questions they ask. They say things like "Will I make real money next week?" The Oracle says, "Yeah, sure," and they get disappointed when they only make a dime. But a dime is real money—not much real money, but real money all the same.

See what I'm getting at? The Oracle will always answer the question you asked, not the question you *think* you asked. So it's worth spending time getting the question exactly right. It's also a good idea to *write it down*. That way you'll be able to check exactly what you asked if things get confused later.

Having asked your question and written it down, lay out your cloth circle on a convenient surface, like a table or floor. Put your three dice into a box, close your eyes, and mentally chant "Wizard's Work, Wizard's Work. Oracle, please answer true." (Magic works from the inside out, remember.) Now shake the box three times with your left hand, make a mysterious smile, and throw the dice onto your cloth without opening your eyes. This may require a little practice, but that's how you get to Carnegie Hall.

To find your answer, you need to make a note of where the dice have fallen—inside or outside the circle—and what number you've scored. You find out what number you've scored by adding together the uppermost number on each die. Your answer will be somewhere between 3 and 18. (I can predict that because I'm a very experienced Wizard.)

Right, now let's look at the way the Wizard's Oracle gives answers to your questions. First, we'll note how many dice fell inside your circle and how many outside.

All outside the circle: You will probably get what you want, but in the long term this will prove to be a bad thing.

Two outside the circle: Watch out for a bad quarrel that will have an effect on this.

One outside the circle: It doesn't matter what else the Oracle shows, you'll find there will be enormous problems in carrying this through. (But it *is* possible.) Now let's have a look at what the scores mean:

3   Some surprises predicted here. And very soon.

4   You're well advised not to go on, otherwise unpleasantness will result.

5   You'll get help on this from somebody you don't know yet.

6   Sorry, but you're likely to suffer loss in connection with this matter.

7   Hassles and gossip will interfere with what you want to do.

8   You'll be criticized and blamed if you go on.

9   The friendship of somebody you know will affect this.

10   Something new—possibly even a birth—will influence the thing you're asking about and you shouldn't take action until you discover what this is.

11   This will be influenced by a parting from somebody you care about.

12   You'll get your answer soon by letter or e-mail.

13   Don't go on with this or you'll be very sorry.

14   A new friend will help you.

15   There's trouble ahead so proceed with extreme caution.

16   You, or somebody concerned, will make a journey in connection with this and the result will be very happy indeed.

17 This will come out okay for you.

18 Hey, wow, this is going to be great. You're going to be successful and everybody's going to benefit. Soon, too.

You can stop right there and still get a useful answer from the Oracle. And I'd advise you to do just that until you get the hang of it and start learning what the various numbers mean. If you use the Oracle often, it won't be long before you can make a consultation without having to look up the answers in this book. Once you reach that stage, you can go on to using the full Oracle, which takes account of the numbered sectors.

Throw the Oracle dice exactly as you did before, but this time, note which sectors now have dice in them and add the sector meaning to your answers.

Here are what the twelve sectors are all about:

Sector	What It Refers To
1	The next 365 days.
2	Money matters.
3	Travel.
4	Your home or where you happen to be at the moment. This isn't just your house—it could refer to your town or general environment.
5	Anything you're working on at the moment.
6	Health, including medical matters.
7	Partnerships, romances, marriages.

8	Deaths, massive changes, legacies.
9	Your state of mind.
10	What you do—this could be your job if you have one, or the fact you're a student.
11	Friends.
12	Enemies.

Might seem a bit complicated at first, but after a while, you'll find it all comes naturally to you and you'll use the Wizard's Oracle like a real Wizard.

TASK FOR LESSON EIGHT

Make up a Wizard's Oracle and ask it if you should go on to Lesson Nine.

Lesson Nine:
Star Magic

The other night I watched some idiot on television say that if it wasn't for bad luck, he'd have no luck at all.

Well, I've no time for that sort of attitude I can tell you. No time at all. If you're suffering from bad luck, or the Wizard's Oracle predicts a tricky time ahead, *do something about it!* That's the Wizard's Way. You're not here to be pushed around by Fate. You're here to take charge of your life, and that includes taking charge of your luck.

There are lots of ways you can do it and since most of them have to do with the planets and the stars—what Wizards call *astrology*—you have to learn the basics of that first. I'm not going to make you set up a horoscope or anything complicated—just give you enough so you have something to help you understand people (including yourself), and work the magic you'll need to change your luck.

Okay, here goes.

The most important thing in the sky is the Sun. If it went out tomorrow, you'd be dead by Thursday and so would everybody else. Your Sun Sign (which means where the Sun was when you were born) is the major influence on the type of person you are. That means you can tell something about the sort of person anybody is once you learn when they were born.

There are twelve Sun Signs altogether. Here are their names, dates, and special symbols. You don't have to learn them by heart to become a Wizard. Just look them up when you need them.

Name	**Symbol**	**Dates**
Aries, *the Ram*	♈	March 21–April 20
Taurus, *the Bull*	♉	April 21–May 20
Gemini, *the Twins*	♊	May 21–June 20
Cancer, *the Crab*	♋	June 21–July 21
Leo, *the Lion*	♌	July 22–August 21
Virgo, *the Maiden*	♍	August 22–September 22
Libra, *the Scales*	♎	September 23–October 22
Scorpio, *the Scorpion*	♏	October 23–November 22

Name	Symbol	Dates
Sagittarius, the Archer	♐	November 23–December 20
Capricorn, the Goat	♑	December 21–January 19
Aquarius, the Water-carrier	♒	January 20–February 18
Pisces, the Fish	♓	February 19–March 20

With this table, you can find out anybody's Sign just by asking them their birth date. But a fat lot of good that'll do you if you don't know what each Sign means. So I'm going to tell you enough to get started.

Sign and What Sort of Person You Are
Aries

Good points: energetic, enthusiastic, brave, optimistic, and sincere.

Bad points: reckless, extravagant, impatient, bad-tempered, big ego, boastful, stubborn, sometimes violent.

Type: confident, aggressive, independent, competitive, ingenious.

Likely occupation: military, police, fire service, engineering, or anything using tools, including surgery.

Perfect partner: Leo or Sagittarius

Taurus

Good points: patient, honorable, imperturbable, kindly, and persevering.

Bad points: obstinate, cheap, slow, overly conservative, and overly indulgent.

Type: patient, thorough, constructive, steadfast, persistent, materialistic.

Likely occupation: agriculture, construction industry, acting, clothing, confectionary or jewellery business.

Perfect partner: Virgo or Capricorn

Gemini

Good points: ingenious, versatile, inventive, artistic, sensitive, charming, and generous.

Bad points: unstable, extravagant, tactless, unsettled, sometimes disloyal.

Type: adaptable, selective, analytical, often brilliant.

Likely occupation: literary work, education, languages, sales.

Perfect partner: Libra or Aquarius

Cancer

Good points: sympathetic, loyal, patient, imaginative, generous, serene and faithful.

Bad points: absolutely none whatsoever.*

Type: genius.**

Likely occupation: Wizard.†

Perfect partner: Scorpio or Pisces

---

* Editor's Note: This nonsense may be due to the fact that the Honorable Mr. Rumstuckle is himself a double Cancerian—Sun and Moon both in Cancer. In fact, Cancerian bad points are: irritability, frivolity, procrastination, dreaminess, pride, and morbid tendencies.

** Editor's Note: Unlikely. The more typical Cancerian type is receptive but conservative, persistent but reserved, and broody but sympathetic.

† Editor's Note: Well, yes, but also religion, the sea, institutional work, and any business or profession that involves liquids.

Leo

Good points: big-heartedness, commanding, optimistic, faithful, tolerant, ambitious.

Bad points: pompous, self-indulgent, bossy, hyper-conservative.

Type: generous, cheerful, self-sacrificing, open, and bold.

Likely occupation: management, legal profession, finance.

Perfect partner: Aries or Sagittarius

Virgo

Good points: intuitive, versatile, honest, prudent, quick-thinking, loyal, tactful, and charming.

Bad points: selfish, unsympathetic, calculating, officious, nervous.

Type: investigative and ingenious, skeptical and critical, penetrating, and introspective.

Likely occupation: books, journalism, psychology, statistics, science.

Perfect partner: Taurus or Capricorn

Libra

Good points: balanced, kindly, truthful, respectful, adaptable, orderly, and impartial.

Bad points: hesitant, timid, vain, sentimental, overly sensual.

Type: judicious, persuasive, materialistic, and self-pitying.

Likely occupation: law, diplomacy, finance, navigation, architecture, poetry and literature.

Perfect partner: Aquarius or Gemini

Scorpio

Good points: thorough, cautious, brave, responsible, good
concentration, and strength of purpose.

Bad points: suspicious, callous, cunning, poor judgment.

Type: scientific, temperamental, and secretive. Can be
tyrannical at times.

Likely occupation: police or detective work, chemistry,
surgery, military.

Perfect partner: Pisces or Cancer

Sagittarius

Good points: independent, vigorous, sporting, popular,
honest, optimistic, quick-thinking, and philosophical.

Bad points: overly confident, one-sided, argumentative.

Type: happy, good-natured, flamboyant, and ambitious.
Intelligent and kindly.

Likely occupation: sports, law, outdoors, banking, teaching,
public speaking, ministry.

Perfect partner: Aries or Leo

Capricorn

Good points: ambitious, cautious, tactful, loyal, disciplined,
diplomatic, hard-working, persevering.

Bad points: bigoted, domineering, gloomy, unscrupulous,
limited, arrogant, sometimes cruel.

Type: forceful and concentrated with a love of detail, order,
and organization. Egotistical and fatalistic.

Likely occupation: business organization, building, mining,
agriculture, realty, higher education.

Perfect partner: Taurus or Virgo

Aquarius

Good points: stable, truthful, patient, penetrating, sincere, friendly, calm, and spiritual.

Bad points: indecisive, dreamy, impractical, fixed, overly sentimental, and skeptical.

Type: scientific, inventive, diplomatic and tolerant.

Likely occupation: radio, electrical work, aviation, charitable and social work, science.

Perfect partner: Gemini or Libra

Pisces

Good points: imaginative, idealistic, warm, forgiving, lovable, intelligent, inspired.

Bad points: unbusinesslike, lazy, overly generous, over-anxious, overly sensitive.

Type: idealistic and romantic, creative, and sympathetic.

Likely occupation: entertainment, medicine, literature, the arts, the sea.

Perfect partner: Cancer or Scorpio

What you have there is only a rough guide, of course. There's no way you can divide billions of human beings into twelve classes and expect everybody to be exactly like their Sign.

As well as Sun Signs, you're going to need to know about the planets.

Each one of the twelve Sun Signs is ruled by a planet. That means they have a special connection. Here's a table you can look up when you need it:

Sun Sign	Sign Is Ruled By . . .
Aries	Mars
Taurus	Venus
Gemini	Mercury
Cancer	The Moon
Leo	The Sun
Virgo	Mercury
Libra	Venus
Scorpio	Mars
Sagittarius	Jupiter
Capricorn	Saturn
Aquarius	Saturn/Uranus
Pisces	Jupiter/Neptune

The Sun and Moon aren't planets, but we're just going to pretend they are, okay?

You'll notice some planets rule more than one Sign. This is because there are only seven planets you can see without a telescope: Sun, Moon, Mercury, Venus, Mars, Jupiter, and Saturn. So when the old astrologers were working out the rulers of the Signs, some of the planets had to double up. That's why certain planets rule more than one Sign. That's also why Aquarius and Pisces each have two ruling planets. Aquarius got Saturn in the old days, just as Pisces got Jupiter.

But then the telescope was invented and the rest of the planets were discovered. Next thing you know, modern astrologers were looking for somewhere to assign Uranus and Neptune (and even Pluto for that matter.) They decided Uranus could rule Aquarius and Neptune could rule Pisces.

I don't know what they decided to do about Pluto, but that won't make any difference to your Wizard work.

Okay, that's enough of long-winded explanations. Just try to remember this. When you know your Sun Signs and your planets, you know enough to start practicing a whole huge heap of Wizardry—including, as you'll see a little later, ways to change your luck.

TASK FOR LESSON NINE

Figure out your Sun Sign and its ruling planet. Do the same for your best friend. See if the girl (or boy) you like would be a perfect match. Find out how you'd get along with your favorite pop or movie star.

Lesson Ten:
Magic Times

There is a tide in the affairs of men,
Which, taken at the flood, leads on to fortune;
Omitted, all the voyage of their life
Is bound in shallows and in miseries.

Who said that then? No, it wasn't me. You know perfectly well it was William Shakespeare. Or Billy, as I used to call him. *Julius Caesar,* Act IV, Scene III, to be exact. Well, you're going to learn how to calculate that tide, so you'll never miss the boat again.

The difference between success and failure in Wizardry is often nothing more than timing. Take Moon phase, for example. Generally speaking, it's best to work Wizardry during a waxing Moon—that's when it's getting bigger, night by night, as it moves toward Full.

But that's only generally speaking. You have to take into account the sort of Wizardry you're working. If you were working a spell to bring in a bit of money, then that rule certainly holds. But if you were trying to make your schoolteacher go bald, you might be better working on a waning Moon, after it's been full and is getting smaller night by night.

Can you see the difference? The money spell is all about *more*. The "Make-Teach-a-Baldy" spell is all about *less*. (Not that a good Wizard would waste time on such a petty spell.)

Actually, Moon phase is a very general indicator. An experienced Wizard watches for the New Moon. The fourteen days between New Moon and Full (waxing) tend to be quite good for business, whether magic is directly involved or not. After Full Moon, the next fourteen days (waning) are better for finishing off stuff you started earlier. If you want to get a bit more specific, then you should know that the 6th, 11th, 20th, and 25th days after the day of any New Moon are particularly good for Wizardry of any sort.

I'd avoid the Full Moon itself, though. Sun and Moon are directly in opposition then and that has a funny effect on people. Some of my best friends are werewolves, but I wouldn't want to make a potion with one of them chewing on my leg. Even if you don't know any werewolves, you'll find many of your friends are jittery and quarrelsome at Full Moon. Apart from which, things just plain seem to go wrong then.

I'd also avoid the dark of the Moon, the time when there's no Moon at all in the sky. It's not impossible to work Wizardry then, but it is difficult. Best avoid it until you have a bit of experience under your belt.

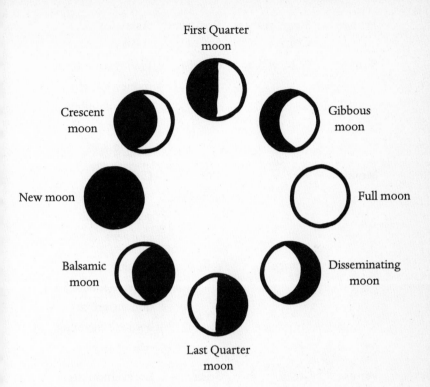

First Quarter
moon

Gibbous
moon

Crescent
moon

Full moon

New moon

Disseminating
moon

Balsamic
moon

Last Quarter
moon

But all this is rule of thumb, just a rough, rough guide to get you started. The thing is, specific Wizardry needs specific times. And the way you decide what times are best is through the planets.

In the last lesson, I mentioned that certain planets are associated with certain Signs. But they're associated with other things as well. Here are the basics. With the basics, you can often make other associations.

Planet	Negative Color	Positive Color	Associated with . . .
Sun	Gold, yellow	Orange	Power, success, life, money, growth, health, illumination, bosses or superiors.
Moon	Puce	Blue	Change, the senses, women, general public, journeys.
Mercury	Orange	Yellow	Writing, business, contracts, information, neighbors, books, bargaining, selling, buying.
Venus	Green	Green	Love, emotions, young people, women, luxury, beauty, the arts, music, social occasions.
Mars	Red	Red	War, energy, anger, destruction, construction, danger, surgery, will power.

| **Jupiter** | Blue | Purple | Growth, abundance, expansion, luck, gambling, generosity, travel. |
| **Saturn** | Black | Indigo | Debts, agriculture, death, wills, real estate, stability, inertia, old people. |

(You'll notice Mars is associated with both destruction and construction. What's that all about? Well, it's all about the way you use the Martian energies. And it's also about the fact that very often you have to pull something down before you build something new. That could apply to old habits just as easily as old houses.)

Now you know the sort of things that are associated with the seven planets, I can start teaching you how to do something about your luck.

TASK FOR LESSON TEN

Figure out which planet would be associated with these things:

1. Getting your tonsils out.
2. Opening a candy shop.
3. Winning the lottery.
4. Writing a poem.

Write the answers in your Wizard's Journal.

Lesson Eleven:
The Wizard's Talisman

One of the simplest ways of changing your luck is to make yourself a talisman. That's a particular object—could be a ring, could be a stone, could be a pouch around your neck—that has the magic to bring you luck. Like all magic, talismans work from the inside out. The effort you put into making one means you take it seriously, so it has an influence on your mind. With your mind tuned in to better luck, you send out signals that attract it. Next thing you know, you're getting better luck.

You'll notice I said *make* the talisman. You can buy all sorts of "lucky" junk, but most of it isn't worth the plastic it's stamped out on. There are only three types of talisman that have even half a chance of working properly.

The first is any talisman made by a Wizard who knows what (s)he's doing. Like me, for instance. That has a broadly based beneficial effect and, while it isn't the best, it can certainly be helpful.

The second is a talisman made specially for you by a Wizard who knows what (s)he's doing. This is far better, because it takes you into account and is custom made for your particular needs.

The third is a talisman you make yourself. And that's best of all, even if you're only a beginner Wizard, because in making the talisman you actually change yourself. In changing yourself, you change your luck.

Here's one dead-easy way to make yourself a talisman. Go take a walk and keep your eyes open. What you're looking for is a stone. By which I mean a pebble, not a rock. And not just any pebble, but a pebble that calls out to you. By which I mean a pebble that suddenly catches your eye, makes itself noticeable. It might be a pretty pebble, or an odd pebble, or a strange pebble, or a weird pebble, but it will definitely be a pebble that really takes your fancy.

If you don't find your pebble first time out, don't worry. Just keep your eyes open next time you go, and the next time, and the time after that if necessary. Sooner or later you'll find your stone. (Or it will find you, as we Wizards like to say.)

When you find it, mysteriously smile, then paint it!

Decide what design you'd like to put on the stone, then paint it. Use your imagination. Use your creativity. Make it as simple or as fancy as you like. It's your stone and you're doing this for you, not to show somebody, not for an examination.

When you have painted your stone and the paint has dried, you've got your talisman. Actually you've got a soul-stone, which is a really good talisman to have. Carry it with you in your pocket, talk to it when you're lonely, and see how much difference that stone makes to your life. (But it's probably best not to mention it to anybody who doesn't think you're nuts already.)

That's the simplest talisman and it's a good one, but what I really want to do just now is teach you how to make the Wizard's Talisman, which draws on stuff you learned in the last couple of lessons, and is one of the most powerful luck-bringers on the planet. (It also gives you some practical experience in the first principles of magic, which is no bad thing.)

Before you start, you need to go back to the Lesson Nine and figure out your Ruling Planet, if you haven't already done that. To recap, find your Sun Sign from your birthday.* Then find the Ruling Planet of that Sun Sign. That's your Ruling Planet, too.

There are three elements in the Wizard's Talisman—the Planetary Sigil, the Planetary Square, and the Planetary Herb.

I'll tell you about the Planetary Sigil first.

Every one of the seven visible planets has a particular symbol. Each symbol is a bit like a printed circuit or a wiring diagram—it shows the way the energy flows in the particular planet. For thousands of years, these diagrams were very, very secret. (You can see why. With the circuit diagram and a bit of know-how, you can make some dangerous machines.) I'm not saying you couldn't get hold of one, but it was difficult and there was a time when just having one about your person could get you burned at the stake.

---

* If you've forgotten your birthday, ask your parents—the horror of it will be engraved on their memories forever.

Then, in 1801, an English Wizard named Francis Barrett (or Frankie, as I used to call him) wrote a book called *The Magus or Celestial Intelligencer.* He printed up some copies and gave them out to those few people with enough intelligence and Wizardry experience to understand them. On the title page of my copy, it says the book is "illustrated by a great variety of Beautiful Figures, Types, Letters, Seals, Images, Magic Characters, &c." Among these, large as life, were the Theban Alphabet of Honorious (given as an appendix to this book, which you should read sometime soon) and circuit diagram Sigils of each planet.

So it's thanks to the Wizard Frankie that I can teach them to you now.

Here are the Sigils of the Seven Planets:

Planet	Sigil
Sun	

| Moon | |

| Mercury | |

Planet   **Sigil**

Venus

Mars

Jupiter

Saturn

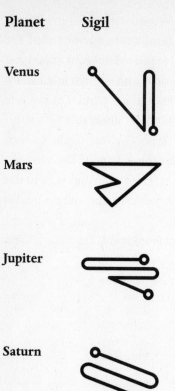

You can make a simple talisman using the Planetary Sigil on its own. Draw it out carefully on a piece of paper (or trace it from this book if you like), fold it, seal it closed with tape, and Bob's your uncle—instant talisman. But you don't want to do that. You want to make the Wizard's Talisman. So I'd better tell you about Magic Squares.

A Magic Square is a grid of numbers that usually (but not always) sum to the same total whether you add them horizontally or vertically. Here's a very simple Magic Square I made up as an example:

```
3  2  7
6  3  3
3  7  2
```

Try it. Whichever way you add it up, the answer is always 12. Some really, really clever Magic Squares add up to the same total along the diagonals as well. Not that one, though. And not the Squares you'll need for your Wizard's Talisman.

Certain Squares carry the energies of the planets just the way the Sigils do. Here they are:

Sun

```
 6  32   3  34  35   1
 7  11  27  28   8  30
19  14  16  15  23  24
18  20  22  21  17  13
25  29  10   9  26  12
36   5  33   4   2  31
```

Moon

```
37  78  29  70  21  62  13  54   5
 6  38  79  30  71  22  63  14  46
47   7  39  80  31  72  23  55  15
16  48   8  40  81  32  64  24  56
57  17  49   9  41  73  33  65  25
26  58  18  50   1  42  74  34  66
67  27  59  10  51   2  43  75  35
36  68  19  60  11  52   3  44  76
77  28  69  20  61  12  53   4  45
```

Mercury

8	18	59	9	64	62	63	1
49	15	14	52	53	11	10	56
41	23	22	44	45	19	12	48
32	34	35	29	28	38	39	25
40	26	27	37	36	30	31	33
17	47	4	20	21	43	42	24
9	55	54	12	13	51	50	16
64	2	3	61	60	6	7	57

Venus

22	47	16	41	10	35	4
5	13	48	17	42	11	29
30	6	24	49	18	36	12
13	31	7	25	43	19	37
38	14	32	1	26	44	20
21	39	8	33	2	27	45
46	15	40	9	34	3	28

Mars

11	24	7	20	3
4	12	25	8	16
17	5	13	21	9
10	18	1	14	22
23	6	19	2	15

Jupiter

4	14	15	1
9	7	6	12
5	11	10	8
16	2	3	13

Saturn

6	1	8
7	5	3
2	9	4

The third element of the Wizard's Talisman is herbal. Back in the bad old days before doctors discovered all the lovely chemicals they have now, they used to try to cure you using herbs and vegetables. Since all medicine was based on astrology then, somebody had to figure out which plants were ruled by what planet. The Wizards managed it, of course, with the result that I can now tell the secret to you. Here's a list of the easy-to-find stuff associated with each planet:

Sun: almond, angelica, camomile, eyebright, juniper, mustard, rosemary, rue, saffron, walnut.

Moon: cabbage, cucumber, cress, lettuce, pumpkin, saxifrage.

Mercury: caraway, carrot, dill, chicory, hazelnut, lavender, licorice, mulberry, oat, parsley.

Venus: cherries, chestnut, elder, gooseberry, marshmallow (it's a plant, really!), mint, raspberry, strawberry, wheat.

Mars: aloes, cress, catmint, garlic, honeysuckle, hops, horseradish, leeks, onion, rhubarb, tobacco.

Jupiter: aniseed, apricot, asparagus, beetroot, fig, hyssop, sage.

Saturn: barley, comfrey, quince, rye, thistle.

Right, that's the basic information you need. Here's how to make your Wizard's Talisman:

Take a sheet of plain paper an inch or two square so that you can carry it comfortably with you. Paint or draw the correct planetary Sigil on one side of the sheet and the Magic Square of the planet on the other.

If, for example, you were born on November 30, your Sun Sign would be Sagittarius and your ruling planet Jupiter. That means you draw or paint the Sigil of Jupiter on one side and the Magic Square of Jupiter on the other.

Now select one plant from the list of those ruled by your planet. In the case of Jupiter you have aniseed, apricot, asparagus, beetroot, fig, hyssop, and sage to pick from. Take a small portion of this plant and put it in a pouch or envelope with your talisman.

That's it. Your talisman is now made and ready for action. As you carry it with you, it acts as a focus for the planetary energies best suited to bring luck in your direction.

TASK FOR LESSON ELEVEN

Make yourself a Wizard's Talisman, then—lucky you—you get to do some more mathematics in the next lesson.

Lesson Twelve:
Wizard's Destiny

Well, it may be math, but it's *simple* math. No worse than the stuff you do at school. Much the same in fact. Just adding up and reducing down until you end up with a single figure. But this time, instead of using numbers to answer questions, we're going to use them to figure out your Years of Destiny. By which I mean the really good years that are coming up for you, the years that offer the greatest possibilities for the things you want to do.

Once you get the hang of this system, you can also use it to figure out the good years for your friends.

Okay, let's get straight to it. Write down your date of birth. In numbers. Like this:

First, write down the day of the month that you were born. Let's suppose you mysteriously smiled and popped into this world on August 7, 1985. The day of the month is 7, so you write down 7.

Now underneath that, write the number of the month. August is the eighth month, so you write down 8. If you'd been born in January, you'd have written 1; if you were born in December you'd have written 12. This is so simple I can't think why I'm bothering to tell you.

Now underneath those two, write down the year. If you really were born on August 7, 1985, you'll now have written:

7

8

1985

Now draw a line under them and add them up. Oh, all right, use your calculator if you have to. Didn't have calculators in my younger days. Oh no, a Wizard had to—well, never mind. In the example above, the total comes neatly to 2000. You have to reduce that to a single number the way you did earlier, by adding the digits in your answer. So, 2 + 0 + 0 + 0 = 2. Easy peasy. Here's another example.

Birth date December 22, 1999.

22

12

1999

Add them up and you get—hold on while I find my calculator—you get 2033. Add the digits to get a single number and you get 8.

The single number you end up with is your Destiny Number. To find the really unutterably brilliant perfect years ahead for you, just check this table:

Destiny Number	Special Years
1	2008 2017 2026
	2035 2044 2053
2	2009 2018 2027
	2036 2045 2054
3	2010 2019 2028
	2037 2046 2055
4	2002 2011 2020
	2029 2038 2047
5	2003 2012 2021
	2030 2039 2048
6	2004 2013 2022
	2031 2040 2049
7	2005 2014 2023
	2032 2041 2050
8	2006 2015 2024
	2033 2042 2051
9	2007 2016 2025
	2034 2043 2052

TASK FOR LESSON TWELVE

Check your Special Years and the Special Years of your closest friend. Then see if you can figure out how to add more Special Years to the table for each Destiny Number and write out the expanded table in your Wizard's Journal.

Have you completed the tasks for the last five lessons? Have you washed behind your ears? If you've read the lessons and completed all five tasks—you can forget about washing behind your ears—make a mysterious smile and chalk up another successful step in your headlong rush toward mastery of the magical arts. You are now, as you sit there grinning, a . . .

Trainee Wizard

in the Second Degree
is Honorarily Conferred Upon

_____

Name

This _____ day of _____

in the year _____

As Recognition of Distinction
in being a Wizard's Apprentice
with license to practice his
or her trade & mystery

Cornelius Rumstuckle

_____

Cornelius Rumstuckle
Wizard Grand Master

Lesson Thirteen:
Wizard's Relaxation

Remember the Theory of Wizardry in your very first lesson? Magic works from the inside out. Take control of what's inside and you take control of what's outside.

One of the things you need to take control of is your daydreaming. You need to make it detailed. You need to make it vivid. You need to make it real.

Here's how you do that:

First, find a place where you won't be disturbed for half an hour. Your room will do if you can get into it with all that mess. Lock the door, put up a DO NOT DISTURB sign, whatever it needs. If you have a phone in there, turn the ringer off.

Next, find a comfortable chair. Don't use a bed—you'll fall asleep. You might even fall asleep in a chair, but we'll have to risk that. Sit in your chair and make yourself comfortable. Make sure your back is well supported (and preferably straight). Now, let yourself relax.

Are you completely relaxed now?

No you're not. You only *think* you are. Nobody except a cat relaxes completely the first time they try it. What you need to learn is the Wizard's Relaxation Sequence. It lets you know what tension feels like so you know what relaxation feels like.

Wizard's Relaxation Sequence

Think of your feet: great, smelly, ugly things.

Now curl your toes down, away from your body. This makes your feet tense. The more you curl your toes, the greater the tension in your feet. Pretty soon this will get uncomfortable, even painful. If you hold it long enough—a few months or a year—your feet will lock up solid and you'll never walk again.

Before that happens, stop curling and let go. Let go completely.

Nice, isn't it? What you were feeling, with your toes curled, was tension. What you're feeling now is relaxation.

Now curl your toes up so they point toward your body, and bring your feet up with them. This creates tension in the calf muscles at the back of your legs. Think about that tension, hold the muscles tense until they start to hurt, then let go. Let go completely.

Now you're feeling relaxed again. Think about the difference between the tension and the relaxation.

Onward and upward to your thighs now. Except my friend the Wizard Gabrielle (an important member of the Wizards' Guild) goes funny if she hears the word "thighs" so Wizards have to call them "upper-lower limbs."

Tense the muscles of your upper-lower limbs. Hold them tight and tense until they feel uncomfortable and then let go. Let go completely. Think about the difference between the tension and the relaxation.

Now your bottom. I know you're sitting on it, but that shouldn't stop you tensing up the muscles. Same as before, hold them tight and tense, then let them go and think about the difference between the tension and the relaxation.

Getting the hang of it now? Good. What I want you to do is continue going up your body in the following sequence, first tensing then relaxing your muscles and always thinking about the difference in feel between the tension and the relaxation:

Your stomach muscles.

Your chest muscles.

Your back muscles.

Your hand muscles. (Curl your fingers to turn your hands into fists, hold it, then let go.)

Your arm muscles.

Your shoulder muscles along the top of your upper back.

Your neck muscles.

All the muscles of your face and jaw. (I hope you took my advice and are practicing the Wizard's Relaxation alone, because you're going to look very silly when you tense the muscles of your face.)

Finally your scalp. Frown to bring the scalp forward—you'll feel the movement if you pay attention—then let go again. Think about the difference in feel between the tension and the relaxation.

By now you should be pretty relaxed, but you can get even more so. Tighten every muscle of your body so you're tense from head to toe. Take a deep breath. Hold the breath and the tension, then let your breath out with a huge, explosive sigh and relax every muscle at the same time. This will relax you even more.

But you can get more relaxed still, and in a very peculiar way. What I want you to do now, sitting there with your eyes closed and feeling very relaxed already, is to imagine the muscles of your body growing long and limp. You can pick a particular muscle or try it with all your muscles all at once, whichever you like. But make your visualization as vivid as you can and watch what happens.

Got you just that little bit more relaxed, didn't it?

That's just your first little hint of how something you imagine can affect the physical world—in this case, the muscles of your body. Here's another demonstration, one you can try out on your friends for a bit of fun:

Sit back, relax, close your eyes, and imagine you have a big juicy lemon in front of you on a plate. Try to see it as clearly as you can in your mind's eye.

Now imagine you have a knife and cut a big wedge out of that lemon. Imagine the tangy lemon smell as the knife cuts through the rind.

Now take that big, fresh, juicy wedge of lemon and imagine yourself biting into it. Imagine the taste of the sharp lemon juice in your mouth. Imagine it pouring down your chin. Imagine the smell and the taste and the feel on your skin.

Now go wipe your mouth—you're drooling. I mean your real mouth, your physical mouth. Making the picture in your mind, visualizing something vividly, did something to your mouth big time.

One more.

You know every so often you get a bottle with a screw top that just won't come off? Or maybe a jar of jam or pickles with a lid that's stuck? You know how you stand there like an idiot, trying and trying, but the stupid thing won't budge?

Try this. Put down the jar or the bottle for a minute. Close your eyes and make a picture of yourself in your mind with huge bulging muscles. See yourself as the strongest man or woman in the world, one of those characters who lifts weights and bends iron bars. Now try shifting the lid again, saying (out loud) *Strong . . . strong . . .* as you do so.

I'm not promising anything, but just try it.

If you don't happen to have a stuck bottle top, you can try it another way. Get a friend to hold his arm out straight from the shoulder. Tell him you're going to try to push it back down to his side and that he's to resist as much as possible.

You should be able to get his arm down with a little effort, but that's not the point. The point is to find out how much effort you need.

Now tell him about visualizing himself with bulging muscles and saying *Strong . . . strong . . .* Try pushing his arm down while he's doing that. You'll notice the difference at once. He really, truly does get stronger. Swap around and try holding your arm out for him to push down.

Later in this book you'll find out how using your imagination can influence things other than your body.

TASK FOR LESSON THIRTEEN

Carnegie Hall time. What you're going to practice is your imagination. Just get comfortable and imagine in sequence the things I've listed below. Don't spend too long on each, otherwise you won't have time to do your homework (as if you cared about that) but do spend long enough to get each image as clear as you can.

As you go through the list, you'll find things get more complicated. You'll start just seeing things in your mind's eye, then go on to hearing and smelling and touching in your imagination. This may seem tricky at first, but it'll get easier with practice. Work your way through the list once to finish this lesson, but if you *really* want to be a Wizard, you'll come back and practice time and again.

Okay, here's the list:

To start with, I want you to see or imagine your own bedroom . . .

Now a sunset . . .

Now a weeping willow tree . . .

Now your shadow stretching out in front of you on the ground.

Sounds now:

I want you to hear somebody singing in a very high voice . . .

Now a car engine starting up . . .

Now a cowbell . . .

Now a thunderstorm.

Tastes next:

I want you to taste chocolate ice cream . . .

Now a nice crisp juicy apple . . .

Now an angel food cake topped with dark chocolate and gobs of whipped cream . . .

Now a potato salad with pickles, eggs, and mayonnaise.

On now to imagining touch:

I want you to imagine the touch of a baby's skin . . .

Now run your hand over the bark of a tree . . .

Feel what it's like when you take a very hot sauna followed by a very cold shower . . .

Dig for buried treasure with your fingers in stony ground.

Next smell:

I'd like you to smell a freshly mown meadow . . .

Now bread baking . . .

Now a farm . . .

Now the kitchen of an Italian restaurant.

Something a bit more complicated coming up— moving images:

You're walking along a beach and look up to see a giant dice falling from the sky toward you. Watch this cube, seeing its different sides as it tumbles down, turning over and over . . .

Now you're standing in a railway station and a train runs past you . . .

Now you're watching a bowling ball as it rolls down the alley and then strikes the pins, knocking them all over . . .

Now imagine a three-ring circus with jugglers, clowns, and a horse jumping through a flaming hoop.

Now something even more complicated:

You're driving down a busy street in summer in an open Cadillac convertible chewing orange-flavored bubble gum and passing a chocolate factory . . .

You're sitting by a stream with your feet in the water. On your right you're holding the hand of a very old man. On your left side you're holding the hand of a young child. Mentally recite a song you know.

Right, that's quite enough imagining for one lesson. On to the next before your head falls off!

Lesson Fourteen:
Wizard's Power

What happens to the music when the radio's turned off?

Nothing happens to it, that's what. It's still there, but you just can't hear it. Everywhere you go, you're surrounded by a sea of radio waves (and television signals, come to that). But you can't see them, can't feel them, can't touch them. You don't know they're there until you actually turn on the set.

Wizard's Power is like that. You're surrounded by a sea of energy that other people just don't know about. That energy is called a lot of different things. Chinese Wizards call it *ch'i*. Tibetan Wizards call it *rlung*. Indian Wizards call it *prana*. Hawaiian Wizards call it *mana*. An old Viennese Wizard once called it *animal magnetism* (honest). It's been called *orgone* and *odic energy* and quite a few other things beside. I call it Wizard's Power. You're about to learn how Wizards handle it.

Here's how you tap into the Wizard's Power:

First, you need to practice breathing. Yes, I know you do it all the time, but you don't do it right. No, you don't. No, really, you—oh, stop hassling and *listen!* When you think about it, if you're surrounded by a sea of energy then you must take energy into your body with every breath. So let's look at the way you breathe.

Sit down now for a minute and just take time to look at the way you breathe. Your chest goes in and out, right? But what happens to your belly? If your chest goes in and out, but your belly just sits there doing nothing, you aren't breathing the way you should be. Breathing with just your chest—which is the way most people do it—is *shallow* breathing. It takes air (and energy, don't forget) into the top of your lungs while the air in the bottom of your lungs quietly goes stale. Which is fairly gross after a few years.

But if you use your belly when you're breathing, if your belly goes in and out with each breath, something else happens. You breathe right down into the bottom of your lungs and you expel the stale air on the out-breath. Try that now. Push your belly out as you breathe in and feel the air moving down into the bottom of your lungs. Pull your belly in as you breathe out and see how you can empty your lungs completely.

Don't overdo it. If you're not used to belly breathing, it can make you dizzy until your body adjusts. Just try a few belly breaths each day, gradually increasing the number until this style of breathing comes naturally to you.

That's only the start, of course. Your next step is to set aside a period of time each day for you to practice making contact with the Wizard's Power. To begin with, I don't want you to spend more than ten minutes at this. But I do want you to set aside those ten minutes every day. That's very important. Ten minutes every day—including weekends—will get you results. An hour or two every time you happen to remember won't get you anything at all. Besides, in the early stages, you have to start small and work up. So ten minutes a day, every day, for the first four weeks. After that you can increase it, slowly and gradually, to twenty minutes a day.

Some Wizards I know have increased it further to half an hour or even longer, but I've never noticed it made them any better Wizards.

Right, you've set aside ten minutes and you're somewhere where you won't be disturbed or hassled by your little sister. What do you do with this time? The first thing you do is relax. Use the Wizard's Relaxation Sequence you learned earlier. Since you're going to do this every day now, you'll quickly find you don't need to go through the whole formal sequence—you'll be able to relax completely right away. But for the first few sessions, go through the complete sequence.

Once you're nice and relaxed, start your belly breathing. Don't strain. It should be free and slow and easy. You'll probably find it tricky at first, but after a while it will get a whole lot easier. Remember you should never strain, the exercise should never feel uncomfortable. Before we go any further, just think for a minute what you're doing. You're surrounded by a sea of Wizard's Power. You take in some of that power with every breath. You always have done this, except that now you're taking in deeper breaths (through belly breathing) so

you're taking in more power. You extract more power from the air you breathe and make sure your body completely expels any stale air (and stale power) that might otherwise remain.

The result of this is that you'll increase both the quantity and quality of the Wizard's Power available to you. And you won't have to take my word for that. You'll feel the energy increase at every session. But while you've increased your supply of Wizard's Power, it's not a lot of good to you because you still don't know how to control it. Here's another important secret of Wizardry:

You can use your finely honed imagination to control the Wizard's Power.

This is where all the hard work you did in the last lesson will start to pay off. When you're really comfortable with your breathing, try this:

Imagine the sea of energy around you. See it as clear, clean, sparkling white light. Take time to watch the billows and the currents. Try to feel the pure, crackling, life-giving energy this represents.

Now, as you breathe in, imagine this white light streaming through your nostrils into your lungs and filling them with clean, clear, sparkling energy. Imagine the light spreading to fill your whole body, making it glow.

Then, as you breathe out, imagine all ills and faults, bad feelings, pains, aches, all the things you want to get rid of, pouring out of your mouth in the form of gray smoke. Note how the sea of light around you takes this smoke and transforms it back into clear, clean energy.

And after you have followed this sequence a few times, note how happy you feel, how energized, how clean.

All this imagining doesn't just plug you in to the Wizard's Power supply. It actually changes the sort of person you are. As you continue to practice—and you should continue to practice on a regular basis for the rest of your life—you will find your energy levels rise. At the same time, you'll find you're calmer, more at ease with yourself. Your health should improve as well.

In other words, you start turning yourself into a proper Wizard.

TASK FOR LESSON FOURTEEN
Turn on the Wizard's Power, baby! Keep a note of your progress in your Wizard's Journal.

Lesson Fifteen:
The Wizard's Mask

This is a short lesson, but tricky.

Ever noticed how you change your personality according to the situation? Of course you do! Don't try to tell me you don't! Do you mean to say you act exactly the same way with your teacher and your friends?

You're not the same person with your mom and with a cop. It's not just you. Everybody puts on a different face at different times. The thing is, a Wizard *knows* he's doing it.

The mask you put on to deal with the world is called your personality or persona. (They both mean the same thing, but psychologists wouldn't get paid as much if they didn't invent new words.) Here's the next big secret:

Wizards put on a special persona to work Wizardry.

Remember I told you Wizardry works from the inside out? What goes on inside your head puts you in charge of what goes on outside it. But a fat lot of good that'll do you if your head is full of hassles the way it normally is. You need to learn to leave your hassles at the door when you want to work Wizardry.

There's a couple of other things.

Wizardry doesn't work all that well without enthusiasm. You need to get yourself hot. One old Wizard advised that you should "inflame yourself with prayer"! Just what I've been telling you, in other words.

And Wizardry won't work at all unless you're confident. Unless you know deep in your dear, sweet, little heart that you're going to succeed. So you need to stop hassling about stuff, you need to get excited (inflamed! inflamed!) and you need to be absolutely, totally, utterly, deep-down confident.

Not easy, is it?

That's not just you—it's not easy for anybody. Even Wizards with several hundred years' experience can find it difficult. What we do is this:

First there's the question of your head. You don't go into an exam with your head working the same way as you'd go into a dance. Not if you want to pass the exam you don't. And you wouldn't go to the drugstore in the same frame of mind you'd climb into a boxing ring. (Unless you've got a very rough drugstore in your neighborhood.)

When you want to work magic, your head is just as important. Magic is like computers: What you get out depends on what you put in. You think Wizardry is just a bit of fun and that's about as much as you'll get out of it. Take it seriously—and that doesn't mean a long face—and you'll get serious results.

So the first thing experienced Wizards do is get their head right. They decide what they want from the magic at hand and go to it with the right sort of attitude.

That attitude becomes part of their Wizard's Persona.

With the attitude in place, they let the excitement build. Magic is an exciting business and however long you work at it, that never really goes away. They start to think about what they're going to do, about all the powers and energies they're going to command, and the excitement comes roaring up. They let it run—you can't be too enthusiastic.

The excitement becomes part of their Wizard's Persona.

They focus on the job at hand. It's not that experienced Wizards don't have hassles. It's just that they decide to put their hassles on hold for as long as it takes to get the spell cast, or whatever it is they've set out to do. Sometimes focus isn't easy, but they work at it.

Focus becomes part of their Wizard's Persona.

Confidence comes with experience, really. At first the best you can do is approach Wizardry with an open mind. Let's try this and see if it works. If your mind is genuinely open and everything else is in place, it will work—especially if you start with simple stuff. When the simple stuff works, that gives you the confidence to go on to something a bit more complicated. When that works, you go on to something more complicated still.

Confidence becomes part of the Wizard's Persona.

That's how you build up your Wizard's Persona, a little at a time. But once you've tied it together, you don't have to worry about the separate bits any more. You put on your Wizard's Persona all of a piece.

Did you catch that? Were you wide awake? You put on the Persona. You pull it over your head like a T-shirt. One minute you're your usual bumbling, simple self. Next minute you're *focused* like a Wizard . . . and it shows. I've watched it hundreds of times. You get a group of Wizards together and they laugh and joke together like any other bunch of idiots. But when it's time to get down to work, they change. Every one of them. They've put on their Wizard's Personas.

One great trick is to put on your Wizard's Persona the same time you put on something else, like your Wizard's Ring or your Wizard's Robes. I'll talk to you about Wizard Rings and Wizard Robes in the next lesson, but you can see how it works.

What it means is that you can link stuff together in your head so that when you do one thing, the other comes up automatically. So if you put on your Wizard's Robes at exactly the same time you put on your Wizard's Persona, and you do it often enough, the time comes when you only have to put on the robes—the Persona follows automatically.

TASK FOR LESSON FIFTEEN
For the next seven days, leave aside ten minutes a day to work on building up your Wizard's Persona. You won't get it perfect in a week, but it's a start.

Lesson Sixteen:
Wizard's Robes, Wizard's Ring

This lesson is even shorter, but a lot less tricky.

In the fairy tales you read as a kid, the Wizard was always dressed up in a pointy hat and shiny silver robes with suns and moons and stars embroidered all over them.

Well, you can forget the pointy hat for a start. The last time I wore a pointy hat was when they stood me in a corner for being at the bottom of the class at school. Here's the next great secret of Wizardry:

No real Wizard ever wears a pointy hat.

You can forget about the shiny silver robes as well. Wizards do wear robes, but if you catch one in shiny silver with embroidered suns and moons, you can bet he's going to a fancy dress party, not heading somewhere to make magic.

Your basic Wizard Robe looks like this:

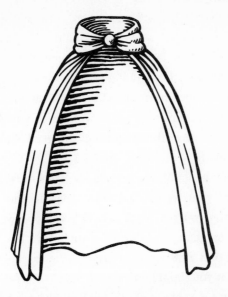

It can be made from cotton, linen, silk, or any other natural material you can reasonably afford. When you put the robe on, you should be covered from your neck to your ankles as you close the robe around you.

There are one or two exceptions when you get into really advanced magical operations, but the color of a working Wizard's Robe will be either plain white or plain black.

A few years ago I heard from a group of Wizards who insisted everybody work in white robes. They had this crazy idea that black robes meant black magic. Well, let me tell you, I've worn black robes since the day I was a baby Wizard and anybody who says I work black magic gets bopped on the nose. It's not the color of your robe that's important—it's the color of your intentions.

The other thing is ornamentation. Some Wizard Conventions you're blinded by the robes. Lamens, sigils, symbols, gems, and crystals. Talk about fancy embroidery! Everybody trying to pretend they're a Big Deal Wizard, High Initiate of This, Great Huge Enormous Master of That. All very well if you're interested in making a spectacle of yourself. But if you just want to work Wizardry, all you need is a plain robe, white or black.

But you could do with a cord—a nice soft white cord to tie around your waist. That's not ornamentation. That's a way to stop yourself tripping over your robe while you're working magic. (Not to be recommended!) My friend the Wizard Lores says white cords are fine for beginners, so that's what you should use.

Why wear a robe at all? I'll tell you. Because a robe helps you cut off from your ordinary day. Put on a robe and you're ready for magical action. It's like a construction worker putting on his or her hard-hat. It gets you in the mood like nothing else can. That's why I mentioned robes in the last lesson about the Wizard's Persona. Putting on your robe makes it twice as easy to put on your Wizard's Persona.

So where do you get a robe? Well, you could ask your parents to make you one. No, honestly. Have another look at that picture. Did you ever see a more simple garment in your life? Not fancy, but workable.

That said, I *bought* my first Wizard's Robe. I found it in a clerical supply store. Nobody asks if you're a vicar. There might be an old Halloween robe about the house you could use. Or you could even forget about a robe altogether and simply decide that you'll always wear particular items of your own clothing when you work magic. The trick is to keep the same clothes for your Wizardry and *not use them for anything else.*

You don't need a Wizard's Ring. You can go right through your whole magical life and never own a Wizard's Ring. But it sort of nice to have one.

You can make one of those as well—you can make *anything* you need for Wizardry—but there's a better way. The better way is to wait.

Of all the magical items, the Wizard's Ring is the most likely just to turn up one day. You'll know it when you see it. You'll take one look and think, *Wow! I'd like that for my Wizard's Ring.* Could be any sort of ring, even something out of a vending machine. You might end up buying it, or swapping something for it, or maybe someone will give it to you as a gift.

You may have to wait a while, though. I'm still waiting for my Wizard's Ring after more than forty years. I've had some great rings in my time—including an amethyst poison ring I lost before I could poison anybody with it—but none of them have been my Wizard's Ring. It'll turn up one day. Or it won't.

Either way it certainly won't stop me working magic.

TASK FOR LESSON SIXTEEN

Wait patiently for your Wizard's Ring and decide what you want to do about your Wizard's Robe. You don't actually have to make one or buy one—although you can if you wish—but decide which before moving on to the next lesson.

Lesson Seventeen:
Wizard's Space

If you ever become a brain surgeon—no, it could happen—you'd never think of performing an operation without disinfecting the instruments you use and the place where you plan to use them.

Wizards work that way, too. Soon I'll tell you how to "disinfect" your magical instruments—the Wizard's Tools — but in this one I'm going to concentrate on your workspace.

Just like the operating room of the brain surgeon, the Wizard's workspace has to be cleared and, in a sense, disinfected. What you're really doing is setting up a place where your magic has the best possible chance of working effectively. There shouldn't be any stray energies seeping in. There shouldn't be any unwelcome entities creeping around to find out what you're up to.

But if you go back to first principles, back to the first thing I ever taught you, you'll remember that Wizardry works from the inside out. That means there are *two parts* to a Wizard's workspace—the space he's standing in and the counterpart of that space inside his head.

I know that's a tough one, so let me give you an example.

Look around you at the place where you're reading this book. Maybe you're sitting at home, maybe you're lying on the grass in a park. Doesn't matter, just look around wherever you are.

Now close your eyes and make a picture in your mind of the place you've just looked at.

See what's happened? Instead of one place, there are now two places. One is the place where you're reading the book. The other is the replica of it you've just mocked up inside your head.

I got you to do that on purpose just so you'd know what I was talking about, but the fact is you do it all the time without even noticing. It's how you walk around your room in the dark. It's how you find your way around a familiar town. You know what's around each corner before you turn it, you know where each street leads, because you have a mock-up of the town inside your head.

So when we talk about a Wizard's workspace, we're really talking about two workspaces—the physical workspace and the picture of that space inside the Wizard's head.

With me so far? Good.

The only reason I'm making this so complicated is that, unlike the surgeon, it isn't the physical workspace that's important. It's the workspace inside your head. (Which doesn't mean you can neglect the physical space—it needs to be clean and tidy—but the real work is done in your imagination.)

Okay, let's start with the physical. You're planning a little bit of Wizardry and you need somewhere to carry it out. So first find a space large enough to do the work and, hopefully, quiet enough so you won't be disturbed.

Now clear it.

No Wizard works well surrounded by clutter. I'm not telling you to tidy your room—I know how far *that* would get me—but I am telling you to clear yourself a working space. Give yourself elbow room. This may mean picking up a few smelly socks and pushing a couple of chairs to one side. So is that going to kill you?

Now clean it.

I'm not talking mop and bucket here unless you're planning to work in a real pigsty. But I am telling you that dirt attracts things that you don't want attracted. So if the place needs sweeping, sweep it. If it needs polishing, polish it. If it needs washing, wash it. Clear and clean, that's your motto from now on.

A clear, clean space isn't a sacred space, but it's a start. Your next job is to turn the clear space into a sacred space. There are several ways to do this, but by far the best is this:

You know how you always hear about a magic circle? Well, you're going to draw one. And here's another of those fabulous Wizard secrets I keep letting you in on:

A circle becomes magic when you draw it inside your head.

Sit down in the exact center of your working space. Close your eyes and imagine you're closely surrounded by a circle of blue fire. The shade of blue is important. You need to make it a luminous, clear, pale sky blue. Imagine this clear, clean, blue flame burning in a circle right around you.

Now imagine the circle of flame expands outward so it eventually grows to fill your working space. Imagine that as it expands, it burns up all the dirt, leaving the space inside the burning circle—including you—clean as a whistle.

If you've done this properly, you should be left with a clean inner workspace surrounded by a circular wall of clear blue flame.

TASK FOR LESSON SEVENTEEN

Practice setting up an area of sacred space. Note any problems in your Wizard's Journal.

Lesson Eighteen:
A Little Light Wizardry

Are you still doing your Wizard's Power exercises? No excuses. You're supposed to keep those up every day. Every day. How do you think you're going to become a real Wizard if you're not connected to the Wizard's Power?

Besides, you're going to need that power right now. Because you're about to learn a little light Wizardry—magic that goes beyond things like preparing your space or making your Wizard's Tools. I'm going to show you how to get *results* the Wizard Way.

Okay, here we go.

Let's suppose you just sat on your best friend's favorite CD and completely broke it. Your best friend hasn't found out yet, but if you don't replace it soon, that's another nice relationship gone down the tubes. Trouble is, your best friend isn't into good music. The CD you just busted was a rare example of some guy who used to play piano in the Stone Age. You've tried all the local music stores. You've run searches on the Internet. You've come up with zilch. There doesn't seem to be another copy of that CD in the whole known universe.

Time for a little light Wizardry.

Grabbing your well-thumbed copy of *The Book of Wizardry*, you quickly turn to Lesson Ten, where you discover the planet associated with music is Venus.

Ideally, you should figure out the Planetary Hours ruled by Venus, but since you're still just a beginner Wizard, the chances are this little operation could take longer than a Planetary Hour to get results, so I'd advise you to start working the *last thing at night* before you go to bed. That way, you can fall asleep with the Wizardry still running, so to speak, and let the mighty power of your sleeping mind help things along.* If you're *really* keen, you'll repeat the operation first thing in the morning as well.

What you do is this:

Build up the Wizard's Power the way you learned earlier.

Now start to imagine the negative color of Venus—green. As you see the color in your mind's eye, imagine everything around you beginning to glow green with the Venus light.

The result of this is that you draw on yourself all the Venus energies in the universe, starting in motion a great current of secret power that will sweep toward you exactly those things you need to solve your Venus problem (music in the form of the damaged CD).

---

* We'll be talking about the mighty power of your sleeping mind later in this book.

Now this is important. It's no good sitting alone in your room waiting for the CD to fall through your ceiling. Magic just doesn't work like that, whatever you've been reading. *Magic works through natural channels.* That's another of the big Wizardry secrets. And now you know it, you'd better keep those channels open.

By this I mean you should keep trying to find the CD, exactly as before. You should keep calling the stores, keep searching the Net, keep asking friends to help you. The difference now is that, with the power of Wizardry on your side, your efforts will bring results.

(Incidentally, if your best friend had simply lost the CD—nothing to do with your sitting on it—you could have offered her a little Wizard help by changing things slightly. Instead of imagining all the Venus forces converging on you, you would have imagined them projected out from you to your friend. If you were dealing with something other than Venus or Mars energies, you would also need to use the positive color of the planet in this instance.)

Task for Lesson Eighteen

Decide on a project, then, as an experiment, try a little light Wizardry to help you complete it. Note the results you obtain in your Wizard's Journal.

Aren't you doing well! To be honest, I never thought you'd get this far. But you have, which just shows how much I know. At this stage, you've got a great grounding in Wizardry. You've got the gear. You've got the power. You've got the basic technique. If you want to go further, I'm including a few advanced lessons in this book that will take you all the way up to the Wizard's Adventure, the only way you can get to join the Wizards' Guild. But for the moment, you have my permission to call yourself by the elevated title of . . .

Trainee Wizard
in the Third Degree
is Honorarily Conferred Upon

_____

Name

This _____ day of _____

in the year _____

As Recognition of Distinction
in being a Wizard's Apprentice
with license to practice his
or her trade & mystery

Cornelius Rumstuckle

_____

Cornelius Rumstuckle
Wizard Grand Master

Lesson Nineteen:
The Wizard's Secret Art of Memory

Ever wonder how you're going to remember all the stuff you're supposed to? Wizards have to remember more than most, as you've probably gathered by now. In the olden days they had to remember even more. They did a lot of ceremonial work then, full of dreadful, unpronounceable Names of Power, and they had to memorize the lot. What's more, there was an urban legend about that—if you got a single word wrong, something nasty ate you. It wasn't true, but it certainly kept Wizards on their toes.

They tackled the problem in a typical Wizardish sort of way. They stole the secret Art of Memory.

The character they stole it from was a Greek poet named Simonides, who lived more than 2,500 years ago. Sims, as I used to call him, wasted most of his time writing victory odes, dirges, elegies, and all that sort of rubbish. But it got him lots of dinner invitations and one night he was asked to attend a victory banquet.

You haven't lived until you've been to a Greek banquet. It's always been the custom that you take a little wine to relax and halfway through the banquet you're usually so relaxed you can't stand up. That's when they start the dancing. Laugh? I thought I'd never—*hrumph*, well, that's quite far enough down Memory Lane: I was telling you about the banquet old Sims went to.

The floor fell in.

No, really. Killed the lot of them. Mangled corpses all over the place. Except for old Sims, of course. Call of nature, I believe. Anyway, he went off somewhere just before it happened. When he came back, it was like World War III. (Except they hadn't even had a First World War in those days.) Somebody asked him to identify the bodies.

Looked impossible, of course. There were hundreds of guests and most of them were so smashed up their mothers wouldn't have known them. But Simonides smiled mysteriously, because he suddenly realized he could remember everybody who'd been there by visualizing where each guest was sitting.

And that's what inspired him to develop his secret memory system.

Actually, it didn't stay all that secret for long. The trouble was Sims mentioned it to his best friend which, as you probably know, is like putting an ad in the paper. His best friend told her best friend, who told his best friend—all in total confidence, you appreciate—and before you could say Wizardry, it was all over Greece. Then the Romans marched in and took it the way they took everything else.

But the secret went back to being secret after the fall of the Roman Empire. That was followed by the Dark Ages when nobody knew anything about anything. Except the Wizards, of course. They had the old books, you see. Including the books Simonides wrote. They grabbed hold of Sims's system and passed it off as the Wizard's Secret Art of Memory.

The Wizard's Secret Art of Memory is based on something called a *locus*. That means "place" in Latin. But it's a very special sort of place—one that exists in two places at once.

Yes, I know that's confusing. But just stop complaining for a minute and listen. (Did I ever promise you that Wizardry made sense?) Here's an example of somewhere that exists in two places at once . . . *your home!*

Yes, it does. Just listen. Your home exists in bricks and mortar at 78875543321176 East 56th Street, New York, New York, or wherever it is you happen to live. But it also exists inside your head. If I asked you the color of the front door, you could tell me. If I asked what was on top of the piano in the living room, you could tell me. And without going to look either. You carry an image of your home inside your head. Wizards would say you have a physical home and an astral home.

Anywhere that exists in two places at once can be used as a locus in the Wizard's Secret Art of Memory. Take a look at this list and I'll show you how:

Book

Television set

Dinosaur

Vase

Kitten

Photograph

Jeep

The *Rugrats*

Donut

Wand

Lion

Chopsticks

Mount Everest

Guitar

Count Dracula

Egyptian mummy

Hat

Baseball bat

Telephone

Computer

Magazine

DVD player

The president

Airplane

The *Mona Lisa*

Okay, you've read the list. Now turn the book over and write down as many items as you can from memory. I'll wait.

There are twenty-five items on that list. How many did you remember? All twenty-five? Liar, liar, pants on fire! I'd be surprised if you got even half of them. But that's because you haven't used the Wizard's Secret Art of Memory.

Let's try it again. But this time before you even look at your list, I want you to imagine your home. I want you to imagine you're standing at the front door. No, on the outside. As if you were about to come in. Now imagine the first item on the list—the book—on the doorstep. See it as a big book. In fact, see it as a giant book, so you have to climb over it to get into your front door. Or you could imagine it with arms and legs, singing and dancing if you like. In other words, exaggerate the book.

Having placed the book on your front step, try nailing the television set (second item on your list) to the front door. Yes, of course that would ruin the set, but you're only *imagining*, duh! Use a big spike. Imagine the television set squirming. Exaggerate the television set.

Open the front door with the squirming television set and see the dinosaur in your front hall. You don't have to exaggerate a dinosaur—it's exaggerated enough already. Just make sure it doesn't eat you.

Have you got the idea? I don't know what your house is like, so I can't walk you through it. But the idea is to stroll through the rest of your home, placing the items on your list, in order, in the various places you visit. If you've got a really big home, you could place one item in each room. If you're living in a one-bedroom, you'll have to place them in different places around a single room. Doesn't matter which—just do it. And don't forget to exaggerate the items. Make them too big, too small, dancing, or drunk. Exaggerate them any way you want.

What do you mean, you can't fit Mount Everest into your home? Of course you can't fit Mount Everest into your home. You couldn't fit Mount Everest into the White House—it's the biggest mountain in the world. But you can fit it into your *imaginary* home all right. Just stuff it in. And be careful with the Sherpas.

Okay, once you've placed the items from the list in your imaginary home—your *locus*—turn the book over again and let's see how many you remember now. Just close your eyes and imagine yourself walking through your home the way you did before. Only this time, note down the things you find there. Like the book on your front step, the television nailed to the door, the dinosaur in the hall and so on, right the way through to the *Mona Lisa* your parents stole from the Louvre and hung in the bathroom.

I'm not saying you'll remember *every* item on the list—this is the first time you've used the Wizard's Art of Memory after all—but I can guarantee you'll get more right than you did first time. And I can also guarantee that with a little practice, you *will* be able to remember every item on the list, or any other list, with next to no effort whatsoever.

When that happens, you can run through the entire list forward or backward (reverse the direction you go through the house when you want to read it backward). You can also name the fifteenth item on the list, or any other numbered item—simply walk through counting.

It's a good idea to start the Wizard's Art of Memory with your home as a locus, but later on when you want to remember enormous amounts of information, you might want to build a different, bigger locus. The old Wizards of Renaissance Europe used to walk through large public buildings—libraries, museums, that sort of thing—until they knew every inch of them. You can do the same thing with a large public building in your area. It'll make a great locus.

It'll also give you practice for something I want to teach you in the next lesson—the building of your Wizard's Castle. But before we move on to that, here's something you can do to impress your friends. How'd you like to be able to name the day that matches any given date throughout the entire year? Like, I mean, instantly.

Actually it's a trick, although it does require a little memory, but no more than you'll handle easily using your locus.

First you have to do a little preparation. Take the current year's calendar and look for the dates of the *first Sunday* of each month throughout the year. I don't know what year you'll be reading this book, but back in 1996, for example, the first Sunday of January was January 7, February was February 4, March was March 3, April was April 7, May was May 5, and so on.

Write all those numbers down one after the other so you end up with a twelve-digit number. (In 1996 it was 743752741631, but you'll be working with a different number for your current year.) That number is the only thing you actually have to remember. You can manage it quite easily by leaving each digit of the number, in order, in your locus. Be sure to exaggerate the digits. Have the first one in glorious Technicolor®. Have the next dancing a tango. And so on.

Once you're sure you know it by heart, you can challenge a friend to give you a date. Let's suppose it's July 20. Now, pay attention, because I'm going to show you how to figure out the day using the year 1996 as an example.

For 1996, you've memorized the number 743752741631. January is the first month, February the second and if you count on a bit, you'll find July is month seven. So count along the number you've memorized until you reach the seventh digit. Which, by an amazing coincidence, also happens to be 7 in our example. This tells you that the first Sunday in July fell on July 7.

Once you know that, you can figure out the second Sunday falls on July 14, the third on July 21 and the fourth on July 28—just add seven for each week. Since July 21 is a Sunday, it follows that July 20, the date you're looking for, has to be the day before—a Saturday. Easy peasy. Look strained for a while, then smile mysteriously and tell your friend.

TASK FOR LESSON NINETEEN

Set yourself up a locus and work with it until you can perfectly memorize the list I gave you.

Lesson Twenty:
The Wizard's Castle

This is Advanced Wizardry—you're going to build yourself a castle.

How much is that going to cost? Don't you ever stop complaining? It's not going to cost you a penny. Not a cent. All it's going to cost you is a little time and effort. And practice. The way you get to Carnegie Hall, right?

The Wizard's Castle doesn't exist in the physical world. It exists in the astral world. You build it in your imagination, a bit like the locus you were working on in the last lesson. Except there's one important difference. You build your locus on the basis of your home or some other building you knew well. You're going to build your castle on the basis of a blueprint I'll give you.

The blueprint will consist of a trigger description, which will help you visualize a small part of your castle before leaving you to create the rest yourself. When you've read through the description, record it on cassette. (If you don't have a cassette recorder you'll have to get a friend to read it to you aloud until you're used to it.) Then find a place where you won't be disturbed, go through your Wizard's Relaxation Sequence, close your eyes, and play the description.

As you listen to your recording (or your friend's reading) try to visualize your Wizard's Castle as vividly as you can. And don't just see it. Try to hear the sounds, smell the smells, touch the walls and tapestries. Imagine you're walking through the castle, learning what's there, examining the furnishings.

You'll need to do this more than once. In fact, you'll need to do it every day for as long as it takes for you to be able to close your eyes anywhere—bus station, airport, grocery store—and walk straight into your castle.

What you're doing here is building a refuge, an inner working space, a meeting place, and a whole lot more. It's high-class Wizardry, so take the time to do it properly. After the description, I'll tell you how to use your castle. Here's the description now:

You are standing on a grassy lawn outside the towering gray stone walls of a great medieval castle, full of towers and turrets and battlements. This is *your* castle. The flags that fly from the turrets are *your* flags. The insignia upon them is *your* insignia.

No one can enter this castle except on your invitation. No one even knows how to find it unless you tell them. Although there are many other Wizard's Castles in this world, no two are identical. This castle is absolutely and uniquely your own.

As you stand before this mighty place, you can see that it is surrounded by a deep, dark moat, that the gate is lowered and the drawbridge is raised. Only you can call down that drawbridge. Only you can raise that gate. You should do so now, with an act of will and imagination.

You can hear the rattle of chains and gears as the drawbridge slowly descends. You wait until it bridges the moat, then begin to walk slowly across. As you do so, the gate begins to rise as if of its own accord. Once again you can hear the rattle of chains and the creak of gears.

Beyond the gateway is a short, arched tunnel with a series of holes in the roof, and ugly little gargoyles set into the wall beneath each one. You walk through the tunnel with confidence for you know nothing can harm you here—this is your castle, your most secret home.

You emerge from the tunnel into an open courtyard. To your right are stables for your horses. To your left are kennels for your hounds. And directly ahead, towering high above you, is the keep of the castle itself.

You walk toward the great iron-studded wooden door, which opens at your approach, allowing you to enter into a stone-slabbed entrance hall with life-sized marble statues round the wood-paneled walls. Set into those walls, to your right, to your left and directly ahead, are three sturdy wooden doors.

Please step into the entrance hall now. Take a little time to examine and admire the statues, then select one of the three doorways to begin/continue your exploration of your castle.

There are lots of interesting things to find in your castle, among them:

A place of healing
A place of nourishment
A central spiral staircase that will give you
    access to every level of the castle
Secret passages
Dungeons
A chapel or temple

I can't, unfortunately, tell you exactly where these places are within your castle, nor can I tell you exactly what they look like. But I do know they're there, because I've found

them in my own castle and I know other Wizards have found similar places in theirs. So if you explore long enough I can guarantee you'll find them, too. You'll also find chambers even I don't know about, not to mention things you can use in your Wizardry and your life.

Everything you find will be part of who and what you are, because the Wizard's Castle is actually the same as your body and soul. It will allow you to discover things about yourself you never knew, draw on strengths you didn't know you had. You can spend a lifetime in its exploration and never reach the end of it. It is one of the most important tools of Wizardry you will ever use.

TASK FOR LESSON TWENTY

Spend half an hour a day for a week exploring your Wizard's Castle. Note down everything you find there in your Wizard's Journal. Search especially for secret passages—you'll find some open up when you move particular items like suits of armor.

It is very important that you conduct your explorations properly. Walk through the castle in your mind and discover what there is to find. *Don't* simply decide "I'd like a secret passage here" and then visualize it opening; that is an utterly worthless exercise. Concentrate instead on treating your castle as if it were absolutely real and you were its tenant.

Once you get the hang of it, you will find exploring your castle a real pleasure and will want to know more and more about what it contains. Wizards can and do spend years in this exploration, and you could do a lot worse than follow their example. But to begin with, you only need to complete a week before going on to the next lesson.

Lesson Twenty-One:
Wizard Dreaming

Even if you only live to be a hundred, you'll waste thirty-three years and four months fast asleep.

Well, I won't have it. Not with Wizards in my training. Time enough to lie down with your eyes closed when you're dead. While you're still breathing, you can do some work at night, starting with this very lesson. Here comes another Wizardry secret:

Many Wizards do their best work while they're dreaming.

You dream every night. Yes, you do. You may not think it, but that's only because you don't always *remember*. You had your first dream an hour and a half after falling asleep last night. It only lasted about ten minutes, but you had another one between an hour and ninety minutes later. And so on, through the night, with dreams getting longer and more frequent toward morning.

I know that's probably all news to you, but I know about these things.

The first thing you have to do is remember your dreams. That's not hard, but it's not easy either, especially at first. Unfortunately it's necessary, so you can stop complaining. Take your Wizard's Journal to bed with you tonight. And a pen. And a little flashlight if necessary, which it will be if you share your room with anybody else and don't want to get beaten up for switching on the light in the middle of the night.

When you go to bed and before you fall asleep (obviously!) tell yourself that tonight you are going to remember your dreams. Tell yourself it's *important* you remember your dreams.

The trick to doing just that is to write the dream down the instant you wake up. And I mean the very instant—not a minute later, not thirty seconds later, not "I'll just curl up here in my warm blanket for another little bit" later. You have to do it right away. If you don't, I promise you the dream will disappear.

So the very second you wake up, in the middle of the night or in the morning, sit up, switch on your light and write the date and details of your dream in your Wizard's Journal. You can do it in note form if you like, just so long as you do it at once. When you've finished, you can go back to sleep.* The way you sleep, you'll probably only be able to catch one or two dreams a night. But that's all right. I've noticed that once you get the hang of it, you'll tend to catch the really important dreams; the ones that slip away won't matter.

---

* Unless it's morning, of course, when you can't.

All that's simple enough, but in the beginning it won't be all that easy. If you wake up and can't remember a thing, ask yourself these questions:

What was the color of my dream?
What was the feeling of my dream?
What was the shape of my dream?
What was the theme of my dream?

Sometimes these questions are enough to bring the dream back. Returning to the sleep position you woke up in helps a lot, too.

For the first month, that's all you need to do—just catch your dreams and write them down. If you do that each night without fail, you'll find remembering your dreams gets easier and easier. Eventually you'll train yourself so you don't have to make notes to remember any more—you'll be able to tell yourself to remember the dream in the morning and you actually will—but that could take a long time.

Once you get the hang of remembering and recording your dreams, you can start working with them. When you've built up a backlog, the first thing to do is read through them to see if any of them foretold the future. No, I'm not joking. It doesn't happen often, but it does happen sometimes. Dreams really can predict the future. Don't look for big spectacular stuff like meteors colliding with the Earth or plane crashes or wars. If you start predicting those, you're a prophet, not a Wizard. Look for little, unimportant things about yourself and your life, things you dreamed one night and came true a week or so later.

For example, when I was a baby Wizard even younger than you are now, I dreamed about a friend of mine buying fireworks. He turned round from the counter holding three fireworks in a very odd way. Two weeks later, it actually happened. Why did I bother to dream something as silly as that two weeks before it happened? Beats me, but most forecast dreams are like that—little things that don't mean a lot.

The only thing is that a good Wizard watches for them because every so often you *do* dream something in advance that's important.

But don't get hung up about dreams of the future. You may have a few or you may not. Either way, it's not the most important thing you're going to do with your dreams. The most important thing you're going to do is practice some Dream Wizardry.

This particular type of Dream Wizardry was worked out by a tribe of Wizards in Malaysia called the Senoi. If you walked into a Senoi village, you might not think their life was up to much. No big houses, no fancy cars, no TV sets or mobile phones. But when they were investigated in the 1930s, an American scientist discovered this tribe hadn't got into a single war for more than 150 years and hadn't had any crime for even longer. They were one happy bunch of people, and the reason was their Dream Wizardry.

Every Senoi practiced Dream Wizardry from an early age. They learned to remember their dreams, just like you will, but after that they dealt with dreams a very special way. Here's what young Senoi Dream Wizards learned:

1. In dreams you must confront and conquer danger. Always move toward it and fight if necessary. This turns dream

enemies into friends. Recognize that the power of your dream enemies is actually your power, which they have stolen. That means the more powerful your enemy, the more powerful you are. When you defeat an enemy, demand a gift to bring back to the waking world. This can be a song or a poem of a way of doing something. It can be a secret or a suggestion . . . anything, in fact, that will be useful to you in your daytime life.

If you're attacked in a dream by your friends, remember they aren't what they appear. So you can treat them exactly like any other dream enemy. But when you wake up, you should make an extra effort to be nice to those "friends" who attacked you in the dream so the spirit doesn't damage your relationship.

2. In dreams you should always advance toward pleasure. If you enjoy doing something that's bad for you in waking life—like eating two gallons of chocolate ice cream at a sitting—then you should feel free to do it in a dream. It won't make you sick and it won't make you fat.

3. Turn bad dream experiences into good dream experiences. If you find yourself falling in a dream, try turning it into flying. Find out where the spirits want you to go. Explore. Enjoy. Keep a careful lookout for anything you can use in your waking life.

Not difficult, is it? Not difficult at all. Just remember those three things next time you find yourself dreaming and you're practicing Dream Wizardry.

TASK FOR LESSON TWENTY-ONE

Start recording your dreams. After you've done that for a week, you can go on to your final lesson. But you should keep on recording your dreams, and once you find yourself remembering them fairly easily, start applying the three principles of Senoi Dream Wizardry.

Lesson Twenty-Two:
Invoking Merlin

You may have found this out for yourself by now, but there are people wandering about your Wizard's Castle. Other than you, that is. I hope you were polite when you met them. I hope you remembered your manners. Some of those inner people can be very useful to you. But before we go into that, I want to ask you a question:

Who's the most famous Wizard in the world?

Did you say Harry Potter? Don't be silly.

No, it isn't me either, although it's nice of you to think so. It's the Wizard Merlin, of course. Or Merl, as I used to call him. The old boy who brought up King Arthur and did a lot of undercover work to make sure things turned out all right for the Knights of the Round Table. Or as all right as they could turn out.

The Wizard Merlin was part of the "Matter of Britain," which is the collection of stories and magical techniques that underlie that branch of the Western Esoteric Tradition to which Wizardry belongs. He did what Wizards often do: turned into a legend after he died.

I'm not going to teach you how to contact Merlin's ghost—I don't approve of it. But I am going to teach you the next best thing, which is how to contact Merlin's legend— what modern science calls his "archetype." It'll feel much the same as talking to his ghost. You can tell him your problems and ask his advice, which is the whole idea. Here's how you do it:

Find somewhere you won't be disturbed, use the Wizard's Relaxation, close your eyes, and build your Wizard's Castle. Lower the drawbridge and raise the gate. Enter the tunnel.

Count five gargoyles on the tunnel wall to your right. (There's a gargoyle beneath each hole in the ceiling.)

When you reach the fifth gargoyle, take it firmly in both hands and twist it counterclockwise. It may be stiff, but it will turn with a little patience and effort. Once the gargoyle turns, you will hear a noise behind you as a secret door opens in the left-hand wall. Go through the secret door into a short corridor that takes you to an iron-banded wooden door. Open this door using the large latch at shoulder height.

If you've followed these instructions carefully, you'll find yourself in a rather bare stone chamber furnished only with a small table and two chairs set either side of it, facing each other. There are two doors to this chamber, the banded wooden door through which you entered and a locked blue studded door set in the opposite wall. The blue door can only be opened from the other side: It cannot be opened without a key (which you certainly don't have) from the chamber you're in at the moment.

Sit down in the chair nearest to you and wait. Use the time to decide what it is you want to discuss with Merlin, what questions you want to ask him. And let me give you a bit of advice on that. He has no time for frivolity, none at all. If you start asking him stupid questions about who's going to win the Kentucky Derby, I wouldn't be surprised if he stomped off in a huff.

After a little while, the blue door will open and Merlin will come in. You'll know it's him because he'll be wearing white robes and carrying a staff. Not as tall as you might have thought—five foot nine or so on a good day, and thin. Longer beard than mine and more hair, all of it white since he's no longer in the first flush of his youth. Nice eyes. Blue. Both of them.

Stand up politely and wait until he sits down in the chair opposite you, then you can sit down again. Now mysteriously smile and ask him what it is you want to know. Sometimes he'll just right out answer you so that you hear what he says with your mental ear as if you were imagining him talking to you. But he's also perfectly capable of answering you by telepathy, so you suddenly find yourself thinking the answer to your own question. Sometimes he won't talk or send thoughts at all—he'll try to show you what's needed. Very versatile chap, old Merl.

(Oh, and don't call him "Merl." Ever. He hates it.)

It's not a good idea to call on Merlin more than once a week, less if possible. He doesn't like it and if you do it too

often, he just won't come, which is a real nuisance if you really need him. Bear in mind you're asking him for advice. If you ask him to do something for you, he won't. He believes you should get used to doing magic for yourself. So do I.

When your question-and-answer session is over, Merlin will leave by the blue door and lock it behind him. Don't try to follow—you'll just make a fool of yourself.

Once you've made contact with Merlin in the secret chamber of your Wizard's Castle, you can use a shortcut in emergencies *and only in emergencies*. The shortcut is to shut your eyes and clearly visualize yourself in the secret meeting room. You don't need to visualize the castle to get there.

TASK FOR LESSON TWENTY-TWO

Invoke Merlin in your castle exactly as I've just taught you, but the first time ask no questions—just introduce yourself and tell him you hope he'll be able to advise you in the future. If you're polite, he will.

He might even advise you on the Wizard's Adventure.

The Wizard's Adventure

Would you like to join the Wizards' Guild? Would you like to have a certificate that names you as an Accredited Wizard? Would you like to know the Wizard's Secret Code and have a copy of the Special Ritual of Dedication used to bless your Wizard's Tools?

Well, you can't. Not until you complete the Wizard's Adventure. There's just no other way.

Fortunately, you'll enjoy it. The Wizard's Adventure is an examination cunningly enchanted to look like a game. You like games, don't you? Well, you won't be able to tell the difference. The Wizard's Adventure plays like a game from beginning to end. And it's fun, fun, I tell you. Until it kills you, of course. That's no fun at all. If you mess up, you can use your Wizard skills to resurrect yourself and start again.

If—and only if—you complete the Wizard's Adventure, you will discover how to join the Wizards' Guild. That's fun, too. And important if you're really serious about becoming a full-fledged Wizard.

Have you got the nerve to try the Wizard's Adventure? More to the point, have you got the knowledge and the talent? You won't get through it unless you've studied all the lessons in this book. No skipping ahead and trying the adventure without putting in the work. Oh yes, I know what goes through your pointy little head. But cheating won't hack it. First study the lessons. Then try the adventure.

Here's how the adventure works.

Getting Started

To get started, you'll need pen and paper, two ordinary six-sided dice, and your secret weapon.

You've probably got pen and paper already, you can rob your board games for the dice, but you'll have to make your secret weapon. It's a pendulum and this is the first time in seven hundred years I've allowed pendulums in the Wizard's Adventure. So count yourself lucky.

So how do you make a pendulum? All you need is a small weight and a length of thread. Metal beads work well for the weight since they have a hole drilled through them. Wood works well, too, and looks good if you polish it.

Don't use anything too heavy. More than an ounce and the whole thing gets out of control. Half an ounce is usually more than enough. Or less. Fiddle round a bit and see what suits you. Don't use synthetic materials like nylon or plastic—you know how I hate them.

Avoid using thread with a twist. It can start your pendulum spinning and distort the swing. This rules out most of the cotton threads you'll find in your mother's sewing box. Nylon thread, which is stronger, is often a single filament without any twist at all—especially if you have the luck to find a length of fishing line. Yes, I know I just said I hated nylon, but that was for the *weight*. I'll put up with it for the thread.

When you make your pendulum, use a good long length of thread—you'll find out why in a minute.

That's how you make a pendulum, but why would you want to? I'm glad you asked me that. You'd want to because *a pendulum can tap into your special Wizard powers*. Here's how to use it:

Write the word YES on a piece of paper and the word NO on another piece. Set the YES piece at one end of a table and the NO piece at the other. Now hold the end of your pendulum thread in your right hand (or left, if you're left-handed) and let the weight dangle straight down. Use your other hand to steady it, so your pendulum is quite still. Bring it very carefully over the paper with YES written on it and wait until any small swing settles down again.

Now say aloud to your pendulum, "What is your swing for Yes?"

I appreciate you'll feel like an idiot talking to a weight on a bit of thread, but you'll find it's worth it. Just ask, "What is your swing for Yes?" and wait.

Believe this or believe this not, after a minute or two your pendulum will start to move, slowly at first, then faster. It will make one of two movements. It will either swing backward and forward like this:

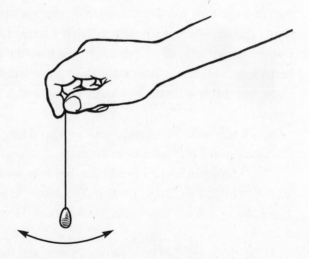

Or else it will swing around in a circle like this:

Make a note of which it does, because that will be your pendulum's swing for Yes. Once you have the Yes swing, steady the pendulum, then ask aloud, "What is your swing for No?" It will show you that one, too.

(If you have trouble getting the pendulum to do anything at all, try shortening or lengthening the thread. That's why I told you to use a long thread. Experiment with different lengths until you find the one that suits you, the one that persuades the pendulum to work for you.)

Once you've found out the Yes/No swings, play around with your pendulum for a while. Ask it simple Yes/No questions. You have to be sure you already know the answers, so they should be questions like, "Do I have a pet dog called Fido?" or "Is my goldfish plotting to strangle me?" Hold the pendulum steady, lean your elbow on the table, and wait.

You'll find it gives you accurate Yes/No answers to these questions.

Even at this point, your pendulum is a useful instrument. But once you get the hang of using it, you can go a lot further. You might, for example, ask it your age and count the number of swings. Or you might write the letters of the alphabet on pieces of paper and arrange them in a circle, then hold the pendulum in the middle and see if you can persuade it to spell out answers to your questions. But that's advanced pendulum work, so you needn't worry if you can't manage it right away—you'll still be able to get through the Wizard's Adventure without it.

How to Play the Adventure

The Wizard's Adventure is an exciting, action-packed story where you are the hero. But you don't read it like a story, starting at the first page and going through to the last. You can't, because it won't make any sense that way.

What you have to do is *get involved*. You have to make decisions. You have to fight fights. You have to overcome monsters. You have to work magic. You have to use your trusty pendulum. You have to roll dice.

You *can* do all that, can't you?

The whole adventure is laid out in sections. You start by reading the first section. But instead of going on to the second section the way you would in a regular story, you'll find you have a choice to make at the end of the first section.

This choice will take you to one of two or three different sections in the adventure. You'll have choices to make there, too, which will take you somewhere else. So instead of reading the adventure the way you would a novel, you bounce through it like a grasshopper, getting more excited by the minute.

No, it's *not* complicated. It's not complicated at all. Once you start, you'll get the hang of it in no time. Just stop being such a worry wart.

In a minute you can begin your adventure. But before you do, you have to learn how to fight.

No, put your fists down, you feisty little trainee Wizard. In the Wizard's Adventure, you fight using dice.

Read the Wizard's Adventure Fight System to find out how.

The Wizard's Adventure Fight System

As you troll merrily through the Wizard's Adventure, you'll meet your fair share of mythical monsters—dragons, manticores, wyverns, that sort of thing. You can outwit some of them by being clever. You can defeat some of them by using magic. But some of them you're just going to have to fight to the death.

Here's how you do that:

Life Points

First, right at the beginning of the Adventure, you have to determine your Life Points. You do that by taking your two dice and rolling them together three times. Add the scores you get as you do so.

You'll end up with a total between 6 and 36. (I know that because I'm a Wizard.)

Make a note of the total because it could represent your beginning Life Points.

Now I'm a fair man and I want to give you the best possible chance of joining the Wizards' Guild, so you can repeat the process two more times. Make a note of the final total each time, then *pick the best score of the three.*

The best of the three is your Beginning Life Points.

Monster Life Points

Anytime you meet a monster in the Wizard's Adventure, the monster's Life Points will be given like this:

"Crouching behind the rock is a two-headed pondoodle-wazzle bird (L.P. 17), which eyes you ferociously . . ."

The *"L.P. 17"* in parentheses after the name of the monster means it has 17 Life Points.

Fighting Monsters

If you decide to fight a monster—or the rotten thing attacks, so you have no option—first roll a single die for the monster, then a single die for yourself. Whoever gets the highest score has first strike. (If you both get the same score, just roll again. And again and again if necessary.)

Once you find out who has first strike, the proper fight can start.

Let's assume you got lucky and it's you who has the first strike. Roll one die and subtract the score you get from the monster's Life Points.

If this brings the monster's Life Points to zero (or less!), then the monster is dead and you can continue with the adventure. If it doesn't, then the monster gets to strike back at you. Roll one die for the monster and subtract the score from *your* Life Points.

If this brings your Life Points to zero or less, then you're dead and have to return to the dreaded Section 13. If it doesn't, then the fight continues until there's a result one way or the other.

Regaining Life Points

When you drop below your beginning Life Points through fighting monsters or getting caught in traps or falling over cliffs or whatever—when, that is, you're injured but not dead—you will regain one Life Point for every new section you visit.

This is a very slow way of getting back your Life Points and if you happen to meet another monster before you're fully up to strength, your chances of survival could be slim. But fortunately there are Healing Potions and other interesting items strewn about the Wizard's Adventure that will allow you to get your Life Points back much faster.

You'll find out about these as you go along. The only thing I need to tell you now is that neither visiting new sections nor taking a Healing Potion can bring your Life Points higher than they were to begin with. But if there are points left over when you take a Healing Potion, you can save these up for later. (You can't save up section visits, however.)

Money

You'll probably need money on your Wizard's Adventure. They don't take dollars where you're going. Or credit cards either for that matter. It's gold or silver or nothing.

Don't panic. I'll *give* you some gold to start you off. Roll your two dice and make a note of the total. That's the number of gold coins you start with. One gold is worth ten silver. (One silver is worth ten copper, but you don't get much for a copper coin these days.) Keep a careful note of any money you may earn/win/find/steal during your adventure. It could be useful for buying things or (occasionally) bribery.

Absolutely Anything Roll

From time to time during your adventure, you might want to try to do something weird or spectacular. To find out the result, use the Absolutely Anything Roll. Throw both dice.

- Score 2 and you failed to do what you tried to do and killed yourself in the attempt.
- Score 3, 4, or 5 and you failed to do what you tried to do and can't try again.
- Score 6, 7, 8, or 9 and you failed to do what you tried to do, but can try just one more time.
- Score 10, 11, or 12 and you succeed.

I think that's about it. If there's anything else, I expect you'll learn it as you go along. So smile mysteriously and turn the page.

Enjoy your adventure and good luck.

Maybe I'll see you in the Wizards' Guild.

Quest
for the
Wizards' Guild

Right, I'm putting a spell on you.

You can resist it if you like. You can simply close this book and forget the whole thing. But if you want to join the Wizards' Guild—if you even only want to find the Wizards' Guild—you'll keep reading and let my spell work on your imagination.

I'm drawing you into a different world. A world with far more Wizardry than the one you're living in now. A world of long ago and far away.

Don't worry, I'm bringing you to a very safe spot in this ancient world. I'm bringing you to the Visitor's Center where you can buy yourself a map, equip yourself with weapons, suit yourself with armor, find a few spell books, and ask directions to the Wizards' Guild. It won't be all that difficult if you just—

Wait a minute—something's wrong! Something's interfering with my spell! You're slipping away from me. You're slipping into the darkness. I can't hold you at all. I can't—

Section 1

You're lying on cold, damp stone. You can hear water dripping in the darkness around you. There is an ache in your shoulder and a stiffness in your legs as you try to clamber to your feet. Even in the darkness, your clothing feels strange—rougher than you're used to . . . and a lot more smelly.

As your eyes slowly adjust to the dark, you can see you are in a gloomy cavern that whispers and echoes to your slightest movement. To the north you can see just the faintest glimmer of light. Behind you, southward, a rock crevice leads into a dark passageway that plunges steeply downward into the bowels of the Earth.

Well, here's a pretty pickle then. But no use complaining. The thing is to decide what you want to do about it. You can follow that glimmer of light at 81. Or squeeze through the crevice into the dark passage at 160. Or explore the cave a little more thoroughly before deciding at 53.

You may use your pendulum to help you decide or work logically, whichever you prefer.

She stares at you for a moment, then sniffs. "Can't say I'm impressed by that," she says. "Not impressed at all. Are you impressed, Harold?"

The Cat shakes his head. "Singularly unimpressed," he says.

You wait for a moment, then ask, "Does this mean you're not going to tell me how to get to the Wizards' Guild?"

She sniffs again. "That's exactly what it means. I'd suggest you do a little revision of your Wizardry lessons before you come back here again. Meanwhile, Harold and I believe you should return to 48 and seek another destination since there is nothing for you here."

You heard the lady. Off you go to Section 48.

Section 3

This looks like a guard post. It's a rickety wooden tower with a lookout platform at the top, high enough to see over the village stockade and for quite a distance across the surrounding countryside. Nobody's going to sneak up on these folks by the look of it.

"Oy, you—clear orf!" a voice calls from above you. "If you don't clear orf right now, I'll come down there and show you myself!"

What an ill-mannered Guard. But then again if he had manners he'd probably be a head waiter and if he had twice as much brains he would be a half-wit. But what are you going to do? You can clear orf back to 48 and pick somewhere else to explore, which would probably be the most sensible option, but if you're not feeling sensible you can wait patiently for the Guard to come down and show you himself at 69.

"No problem there," you say. "Piece of cake, actually. Everybody knows it's Venus, second planet from the Sun, hot enough to melt lead on the surface, sometimes called the Morning Star, sometimes the Evening Star even though it isn't a star. Yes, it's Venus. Definitely Venus. Final answer."

At which point the Sphinx beats you to a pulp, tears you to pieces, cuts your head off, jumps up and down on the bits that are left, and sends you off to 13.

Section 5

Mercifully the passage widens once you get clear of its narrow entrance. Unfortunately, however, it's a lot darker in here than it was in the cave. And as you move cautiously forward, it gets darker still until you can no longer see where you're going at all.

You fumble your way forward, one hand on the rough stone of the wall to your left, wondering if you're ever going to get out of this mess. Then the passage turns sharply right and suddenly you see a dull green glow ahead. At first you think it may be a way out of this passage, but as you draw closer you see it is, in fact, luminous writing scrawled on the stone wall by some long-dead Wizard who has passed this way before.

Even the tiny glow of the script allows you to peer a little way ahead once your eyes adjust and you see to your horror that the passageway splits in three directions. Above the entrance to the first of these the symbol ♐ has been cut into the rock. Above the second is the symbol ♑, while this symbol ♉ appears over the third entrance.

Which is all very well, but which entrance should you pick? Desperately you turn back to the Wizard writing for guidance. The scrawled message reads:

The green road may bring you wealth . . . or death
The black route is death for sure
Only purple will take you where you wish to go

Fat lot of good that is to anybody. Unless they know their Wizardry, of course.

The passage with the symbol ♐ leads to **96**.

The one with ♑ will take you to **41**.

Take ♉ and you'll end up at **20**.

Section 6

This place has location—it's at the center of the village—but very little else. It's a miserable little whitewashed cottage with a thatched roof—which sounds picturesque, but in this case definitely isn't. The walls are dirty and crumbling, the thatch looks as if the birds and wasps have been having a go at it, one window is broken, and there's a sort of open sewer surrounding the whole place like a moat. The smell is absolutely terrible and most of it isn't even coming from the sewer, but from a wizened old Crone in a pointy hat or possibly the black cauldron she's stirring with a broomstick over a small fire outside the front door.

The old Crone looks up and grins at you toothlessly. "Want to come in and have a bite to eat with me?" she asks, nodding towards the cauldron. "I've always been partial to having a nice tender young person for lunch."

Is this old girl for real? And more to the point, are you crazy enough to join her for (or possibly become) lunch at 170? There's nothing to stop you quietly tiptoeing back to 48 to select another destination, which would be a very good idea in my view, but what do I know?

The Priest raises one hand heavenward. "Repeat after me . . ." he says. "Ready?"

"Ready," you repeat.

"You don't have to repeat that—I was only asking if you were ready. Now, repeat after me—okay?"

"Okay," you repeat.

"Are you taking the mick?" he asks.

"Are you taking the mick?" you repeat.

"Look, let's start over," the Priest suggests, exasperated.

"Look, let's start over," you repeat.

"All right! All right! Enough already. May I be cursed with fiery feet and exploding brain if I am a Trainee Wizard!"

"All right! All right! Enough already. Mumble, mutter, rabbit, squinchel, mutter-mutter Trainee Wizard," you repeat.

But will this bit of impromptu Wizardry actually work? Roll one die. Score 6 and your feet catch fire, your brain explodes, and your extremely messy corpse is transported instantly to 13. Score 5 and the Priest's brain explodes, hurling you back to 48. Score anything else and you can move cautiously ahead to 21.

Section 8

"No problem there," you say. "Piece of cake, actually. Everybody knows it's Mercury, planet nearest the Sun, boiling hot on one side, freezing cold on the other, smallish, cratered, bit of a mess really. Yes, it's Mercury. Definitely Mercury. Final answer."

At which point the Sphinx beats you to a pulp, tears you to pieces, cuts your head off, jumps up and down on the bits that are left, and sends you off to 13.

He looks at you delightedly. "This is wonderful," he says. "You're absolutely right. Couldn't be more right if you were ambidextrous. Now here's what I promised you." With that he produces a piece of parchment from a pocket of his robe and hands it across to you with a beaming smile. "Just translate this and follow the instructions," he says. "You'll be a member in no time."

You stare at the parchment in blank amazement:

64383,

55164-0383

Section 10

Well, it's a pleasant enough place—changing rooms, bar, showers, all new stuff—but you can see through the window that the greens look more like a ploughed field and the villagers seem to play with spades and even pitchforks in place of clubs.

Since this clearly is not the place for a serious game, you walk into the bar and order yourself a double sarsaparilla in a dirty glass, then engage the nearest peasant in conversation.

"Tell me, good peasant," you begin, "why might this establishment be called *Wizard Golf*?"

"Because it be a Wizard place to play golf, young master," he replies.

"I don't suppose you know where the Wizards' Guild might be?" you ask.

The peasant rolls his eyes alarmingly and drools. "Do I look like somebody knows where the Wizards' Guild might be?"

He has a point there. Maybe you should just stroll back to 48 and pick another destination. But then again you can never tell with these rural types—they're expert at hiding information. If you have any money left, you could try bribing him at 163. If you haven't, I suppose you could always try to beat it out of him at 125.

This place is distinctly creepy. The inside is even more ruined than it appears from the outside. And those lights you saw seem to flit about from one place to another so that you never really reach them.

There are noises, too. Nothing loud, which, to be honest, adds to the problem. Slithery sounds. Rustlings. Little creaking noises. The occasional hollow laugh—

Hollow laugh? What is this—some sort of ghost story? Look, I'll give you one more chance to get out of here with your whole skin. Just smile mysteriously and creep away quietly to 48 where you can certainly find somewhere that doesn't give us both the creeps. But if you insist on exploring this place further—and risking meeting the hollow laugher—you can do that at 164.

Section 12

The Landlord seats you at a window table and serves you chicken soup, followed by chicken and rice, followed by rice pudding. Then he pours you a soda, after which he carries you (singing loudly to yourself) up a narrow flight of stairs to a room with a low ceiling and a four-poster bed into which you fling yourself and pass out.

You awake next morning with a stomach ache *and* a headache.

That was a real waste of time and no mistake. Get yourself together, then drag yourself to 48 to pick another destination.

Well, that's it then. Another fine mess you got yourself into. You're dead. As a dodo. As a dinosaur. As a coffin nail. If you weren't a Wizard, your only option would be to lie down, fold your arms across your chest, and forget about the Wizards' Guild. (Along with everything else in your life.)

But fortunately you are a Wizard (of sorts), so you can roll up a new set of Beginning Life Points and start all over again. Won't that be fun? Go to 1.

Section 14

"Wrong!" roars the mighty figure before you. "Now you *must* take my advice, for that is the Wizardly law!"

So saying, he waves one huge hand and at once you are taken up and spun around in a vortex of magical enemies. For a moment you feel yourself flying through the stars and galaxies of deep space before you pass painfully through a multiplicity of dimensions to return to a familiar section.

Notably section 48 where you can select a fresh direction or retrace your steps and try a more sensible answer.

"No problem there," you say. "Piece of cake, actually. Everybody knows it's Saturn, sixth planet from the Sun, got rings around it. Negative color black, metal lead, one of the herbs is comfrey. Yes, it's Saturn. Definitely Saturn. Final answer."

At which point the Sphinx beats you to a pulp, tears you to pieces, cuts your head off, jumps up and down on the bits that are left, and sends you off to 13.

Section 16

You press the curious symbol on the wall and at once there is a grinding noise behind the altar. You investigate to find a trap has opened in the floor of the church, revealing a flight of worn stone steps descending into darkness.

You hesitate for a moment before you notice a torch and tinderbox in a wall niche beside the first step. It takes you a little time to figure out the tinderbox, but being a bright young Trainee Wizard you manage it eventually and the torch flares brightly.

Cautiously you step into the secret passage where you are viciously attacked by a giant scorpion that instantly stings you to death.

Oh dear. Go to 13.

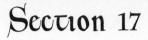

The Blacksmith absently scratches his head with a red-hot iron. "Don't have much truck with that sort of thing myself," he mutters as the smell of burning fills the air. "But there's a Wizard who lives in No. 58—he might be able to tell you. Or failing that, there's an old biddy at No. 6 I've always thought was a Witch. That's some sort of female Wizard, ain't it? Tell you what—if you deliver this Fire Wand I've been repairing for the Wizard, he might feel well disposed toward you."

Your choice as always. You can deliver the Wand to the Wizard at 58 or take your chances with the old biddy who might or might not be a Witch at 6. Or you can ignore all his advice and go back to 48 to find another destination.

Section 18

"No problem there," you say. "Piece of cake, actually. Everybody knows it's the Moon, not really a planet except for magical convenience, Earth's only natural satellite. Neil Armstrong got there first. Gets eclipsed every so often. Waxes and wanes thirteen times a year. Yes, it's the Moon. Definitely the Moon. Final answer."

At which point the Sphinx beats you to a pulp, tears you to pieces, cuts your head off, jumps up and down on the bits that are left, and sends you off to 13.

Section 19

There is a distinct grinding noise as the sarcophagus moves a quarter of an inch, then stops. You wait expectantly, and after a brief pause the grinding starts up again and the sarcophagus moves aside to reveal a short flight of steps down into a passageway.

"There it is," says the Fiend, looking at you delightedly. "Your last few steps to the Wizards' Guild." He waves a gloved hand and the passage illuminates with astral light. "Just follow along until you reach the Guild door. The Doorkeeper will give you your final tests."

Exciting stuff! Don't waste a minute—you're almost there. Follow the passage to **112**.

Section 20

Wow, you could have lucked out here. A short distance along, the passage opens out into a spectacular cavern lit by flaming torches stuck in sconces around the walls. In the center of the floor is a glittering, copper-bound sea chest that looks as if it might be bulging with treasure. This is good news indeed.

The bad news is the chest is guarded by a Winged Lion (L.P. 25) which gets an extra point on each damage roll scored against you on account of the fact that he's just sharpened his claws.

You don't have to do this, you know. You can back up all the way to 5, grinning nervously. But if you want to find out what's in the chest and whether there's some other way out of here, you'll have to fight the lion. If you manage to kill it, go to 113. If it kills you, drop the leading 1 and go to 13.

The Priest leans forward and cautiously examines your head. Then he looks down at your feet. "Not much of a result," he says. "You'd better come in."

You follow him inside the church, which is tastefully illuminated with burning candles.

"Now," says the Priest, "what can I do for you?"

"Actually, I was wondering where to find the Wi—the wah—the wah—the way to—to—to—Carnegie Hall!"

"You want to get to Carnegie Hall?" asks the Priest. "Well, practice!" He roars with laughter and slaps his thigh. "Practice—that's a good one! How to get to—hrumph! Well, if you seriously want to get to Carnegie Hall, there's a secret tunnel underneath the church. Pressing the lion picture on the wall over there will open it up for you."

With which he stalks off, leaving you alone in the church.

You move over to the wall where he pointed, but there's no lion picture to be seen. The only things you can see are three symbols:

Tricky, huh? Perhaps he was pulling your leg about the lion picture. Perhaps your best bet is to backtrack to 48 and select a more sensible direction. But if you want to try pressing one of those symbols, you can push the first of them at 16, the second at 36, and the third at 54.

Section 22

"Wrong!" roars the mighty figure before you. "Now you *must* take my advice, for that is the Wizardly law!"

So saying, he waves one huge hand and at once you are taken up and spun around in a vortex of magical enemies. For a moment you feel yourself flying through the stars and galaxies of deep space before you pass painfully through a multiplicity of dimensions to return to a familiar section.

Notably section 48, where you can select a fresh direction or retrace your steps and try a more sensible answer.

Section 23

What a creepy place. Don't like the look of this at all. First of all, you're in a graveyard where leaning tombstones protrude from barren earth like rotted teeth and lightning-blasted oaks stand stark against the sky, where strange rustling sounds and eerie moans rend the fetid air, where—

But you get the idea. Right in front of you is a towering stone-built crypt guarded by an avenue of granite gargoyles that glare at you malevolently as you walk toward the building.

As you approach the crypt itself, you can make out a faded nameplate beside the wrought-iron gateway that secures the arched entrance. Closer still, you can read the writing. In ornate, Gothic script it says:

Crypt of the Fiend

Through the gate, you can see worn stone steps leading downward into the darkness. The gate itself is, however, heavily secured by three enormous locks, seven bolts, thick chains, and gigantic padlocks.

It is as if someone was determined to keep people out of this ghastly place . . . or to keep something in.

Fortunately not even an **Absolutely Anything Roll** could get you through that gate without a ton of dynamite and a hacksaw. Better get yourself back to 48 and find a destination that isn't going to scare the pants off you. And hurry. I'm not absolutely sure, but I think one of those gargoyles just moved.

Section 24

"Excuse me," you say, "but I've come to the conclusion this is a rather dangerous adventure and I was wondering if you might consider selling me a weapon of some sort, purely for self-defense, of course. An Uzi would do, or even a couple of cannons, perhaps some field artillery, a helicopter gunship, nukes—do you have nukes?—or how about a Magnum? Colt .45? Poisoned stiletto? A few—"

"At your age?" the Blacksmith interrupts. "Are you out of your mind?"

With which he grabs you by the scruff of your neck and marches you back to 48 to select another destination.

Section 25

The little man stares at you for a long moment then slowly shakes his head. "Afraid not," he says dolefully. Then he brightens, "Tell you what. You look like a very nice young person, just the sort we'd welcome in the Wizards' Guild. Why don't you have another try? You know the Wizard's Wing handle isn't blue now, so is it yellow, red, or olive, citrine, russet, and black?"

If you think it's yellow go to 39. If you'd prefer red, go to 56. Or give the olive, citrine, etc., answer at 71.

You twist and turn, turn and twist, return and retwist, coil, wriggle, back up, get confused, unconfuse yourself, snake about a bit, and finally . . .

Emerge at 48. Sorry.

Section 27

You may well live to regret this. Or possibly even die. This is one sheer cliff face and now you're clinging to it with toes and fingertips, the drop seems a long, long way down.

Roll two dice. Score 2 to 9 and the cliff face crumbles, plunging you to your death at 13. Score 10, 11, or 12 and go to 66.

Section 28

"Ah, there you are at last!" exclaims the Apothecary, smugly folding up his broomstick. "I thought you'd never get here. Walk this way."

You follow him across some rough ground with no discernable path until a tall tower looms on the horizon.

"Is that it?" you ask.

"Is what what?"

"Is that the Wizards' Guild?"

"Wha—oh, yes, yes indeed. That's the Guild to be sure. Keep close behind me."

You do indeed keep close behind him, but as you draw closer to the tower it seems increasingly dark and ominous: not at all as you imagined the Wizards' Guild would be. "Are you sure that's the Guild?" you ask.

The Apothecary's face suddenly takes on an extremely unpleasant expression. "Of course it's not the Guild, you little creep! You think getting to the Guild would be this easy? That's the Dark Tower where I can get a very good price for a tender young person like yourself." He takes a Fire Wand from his pocket and points it at your head. "Now come with me and no more nonsense otherwise I shall fill your head full of imaginary fire which will certainly confuse you and might well render you dead, but still palatable to my customers in the Tower."

What a terrible development! To think you've come all this way just to discover you're not really heading for the Wizards' Guild at all. But no use whining about that now. You have to decide whether to follow him quietly at **124** and hope a chance to escape presents itself, run for it at **153**, or make a fight of it at **99**.

As your opponent breathes his last, he transforms back into the Guard you first met. You stand panting for a moment before the heavy scent of magic fills the air and a rumbling sound starts up all around you.

You look up to discover the walls of the bear pit are beginning to cave in, threatening to bury you completely. In something close to panic, you try to scramble out, slipping and sliding as the cave-in turns into a minor avalanche. Can you possibly make it out before the whole thing collapses?

Of course you can, nimble young trainee like yourself. You'll get out easily and in plenty of time to witness the bear pit fill up and disappear completely to be replaced by a nice stretch of camomile lawn as the magic your courage has induced wipes it from the memory of every villager. Nice one—you have my admiration. Now get back to 48 before it goes to your head and find yourself another destination.

Section 30

"Wrong!" roars the mighty figure before you. "Now you *must* take my advice, for that is the Wizardly law!"

So saying, he waves one huge hand and at once you are taken up and spun around in a vortex of magical enemies. For a moment you feel yourself flying through the stars and galaxies of deep space before you pass painfully through a multiplicity of dimensions to return to a familiar section.

Notably section 48 where you can select a fresh direction or retrace your steps and try a more sensible answer.

You've found it! You've found it! It's the Wizards' Guild. Right here on the edge of this dirty village. Look at the sign above the door! How jammy can you get? This was just so easy. Now all you have to do is get in there, find out how to put in your application, and, before you can smile mysteriously, you'll be a fully fledged accredited Wizard of the—

Wait a minute. That sign doesn't say Wizards' Guild. It says Wizard Golf. This isn't Guild Headquarters—it's the village golf club!

What a swiz! But what are you going to do now? If you feel like going in, the door's wide open and leads to 10. If not, you can cut your losses by hurrying back to 48 where you can select another destination.

Section 32

The Landlord shows you to a window table where he serves you a meal of chicken soup, followed by chicken and rice, followed by rice pudding—obviously the "maximize-your-profits" menu. But it's tasty enough and the portions are enormous so you have no complaints.

As you finish, he turns up at your elbow and mutters something about needing the table now, so you belch loudly in appreciation of the food and leave the premises without further ado.

We could have done without that belch. But never mind about that now. Get yourself off to 48 and select another destination.

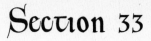

Section 33

You twist and turn, turn and twist, return and retwist, coil, wriggle, back up, get confused, unconfuse yourself, snake about a bit, and finally . . .

Emerge at 48. Sorry.

Section 34

"No problem there," you say. "Piece of cake, actually. Everybody knows it's Jupiter, fifth planet from the Sun, absolutely huge gas giant, has a big red spot that's probably a perpetual storm. Yes, it's Jupiter. Definitely Jupiter. Final answer."

At which point the Sphinx beats you to a pulp, tears you to pieces, cuts your head off, jumps up and down on the bits that are left, and sends you off to 13.

Section 35

"Excuse me," you say, "but I've come to the conclusion this is a rather dangerous adventure and I was wondering if you might consider selling me a piece of armor to help if I happen to get into fights?"

"Well, you're right about the dangers of the Wizard's Adventure," the Blacksmith nods sagely. "Very dangerous business and, if I could, I'd give you every piece of armor in the place, but since I've a wife and seven little blacksmiths to support, I'm afraid money is going to have to change hands. I can let you have a mithral breastplate which blocks 4 points of damage for 25 gold pieces, or an iron breastplate that blocks 3 points of damage for 15 gold pieces. Or I can let you have one of my old string vests that'll block 1 point of damage so long as you don't wash it. That'll only cost you 5 gold pieces. I'll throw in a free healing potion worth a single die roll of Life Points with any purchase. Interested?"

It all comes down to money, doesn't it? Buy what you want if you have the cash or buy nothing if you're broke. Either way, it's back to 48 to find another destination.

Section 36

You press the curious symbol on the wall and at once there is a grinding noise behind the altar. You investigate to find a trap has opened in the floor of the church, revealing a flight of worn stone steps descending into darkness.

You hesitate for a moment before you notice a torch and tinderbox in a wall niche beside the first step. It takes you a little time to figure out the tinderbox, but being a bright young Trainee Wizard you manage it eventually and the torch flares brightly.

Cautiously you step into the secret passage where you are viciously attacked by a giant goat that instantly butts you to death.

Oh dear. Go to 13.

Three minutes after you take off, the Pilot reports engine trouble. Two minutes after that, the rotor blades catch fire. Following which the fuel tank explodes, the Pilot bails out and the whole machine turns into a fireball, which plunges into the waters below.

Red for danger by the looks of that. Climb out of the wreckage on the lake bed and quietly drown at 13.

Section 38

Oh, look—a wishing well! How picturesque. How quaint. It's set right in the middle of the village square, roofed with thatch (the well, not the village square) and looking for all the world like something you'd see in a TV rerun of one of those cheerful 1950s musicals. Except for the signs, of course. There are a series of them set at intervals along the approach to the well. They say things like:

DANGER . . . KEEP AWAY . . . NO ADMITTANCE . . . BEWARE . . . GO BACK . . .

*Looks like somebody's trying to tell you something. But will you listen? You can ignore the warning notices at **120**. Or you can be sensible and return to **48** to find a safer destination.*

"Right!" exclaims the Apothecary. "You're absolutely right—it's yellow, of course. Yellow, yellow, yellow, mellow yellow. Oh, I can't tell you how happy this makes me. Another young Wizard for the Guild. New blood. I love new blood. Now, come this way if you please . . ."

So saying, he leads you into the back room from which he emerged, a small living quarters with a stove in one corner and shelves of books lining every wall.

"Now, my dear young person," says the Apothecary cheerfully, "unknown to most people in this ridiculous village, there is a secret passage from this very room which will take us directly to the entrance of the Wizards' Guild. The opening is behind those bookshelves—those ones there. Unfortunately—" A sheepish look crosses his features. "I have managed to mislay the combination that triggers the mechanism. I wrote down a reminder against such an eventuality, of course—I was never much good at the Wizard's Art of Memory—but now I can't even remember what the reminder means. I wonder if you could help?"

He takes an interesting-looking book called *Magick for Beginners* from the shelf beside him and shakes it until a piece of paper falls out. This he hands to you.

On the paper, in spidery handwriting, is this message:

The friendship of somebody you know will affect this. You'll get help on this from somebody you don't know yet.

"I've done some work on it already," he tells you. "My notes are on the back."

You turn the paper over and find the following:

Maybe double the number of words, add ten, and go to that section? Maybe just give up and go somewhere else entirely. Maybe combine the number of letters in the longest word with the number in the shortest word and go there. My pendulum says it's 102, but I couldn't get that to work. Maybe I should ask the Wizard's Oracle.

What a convoluted mind this old guy has got. If you double the number of words and add ten, it'll take you to section **50**. If you just give up and go somewhere else entirely, I suppose that means returning to 48 and selecting a new destination. The longest word has eight letters and the shortest three, which combined would give you 83. His pendulum says **102** and it might be worth checking that just in case it works better for him than for you. Failing all else, maybe you should look up the Wizard's Oracle and see if you can work out a couple of numbers from the meanings given.

In your panic you stumble on a suspension bridge you never noticed before. Triumphantly you race across it, moving at such a pace you leave even your troubles behind.

Although they will probably catch up with you fairly quickly, since you soon find yourself at 48 preparing to select another destination.

Section 41

The passage darkens as you leave the dull green glow, so that once again you can only feel your way along.

Which you're doing when you plunge into a bottomless pit. You're still falling when you starve to death. Go to 13.

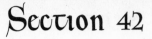

There is a distinct grinding noise as the sarcophagus moves a quarter of an inch, then stops. You wait expectantly, but nothing else happens.

"Well," says the Fiend, looking at you severely, "it seems you don't actually know the spell after all. Call yourself a Trainee Wizard? Call yourself an adventurer? Get back to 48 and don't come back here until you know exactly how many letters are in that spell!" With which he leaps back into his sarcophagus and pulls the lid shut after him.

Better take the Fiend's advice and continue your adventure at 48. Once you find out how many letters there really are in the anti-bear-baiting spell, you can go directly to 82.

Section 43

You twist and turn, turn and twist, return and retwist, coil, wriggle, back up, get confused, unconfuse yourself, snake about a bit, and finally . . .

Emerge at 48. Sorry.

Haven't seen a place like this since I was even younger than you are. What memories it brings back. The smell of molten metal . . . the clink of hammer on the anvil . . . the heat of the furnace . . . the smell of horse sweat . . . marvellous, quite marvellous!

But enough of this reminiscence: you're standing in the doorway of a Blacksmith's forge. Silhouetted against the glow of the fire, you can see the Smith himself, an imposing figure twice your height and half as broad again. He's wearing a leather apron and wielding an enormous hammer. Looks as if he doesn't confine himself to shoeing horses either—there are swords and bits of armor in the racks beside him.

So what do you want to do now? You can simply return to 48, of course, but it might be useful to ask him if he knows where to find the Wizards' Guild, which you can do at 17. Or you could try buying yourself a weapon at 24 or maybe even a piece of armor at 35.

Section 45

"Wrong!" roars the mighty figure before you. "Now you *must* take my advice, for that is the Wizardly law!"

So saying, he waves one huge hand and at once you are taken up and spun around in a vortex of magical enemies. For a moment you feel yourself flying through the stars and galaxies of deep space before you pass painfully through a multiplicity of dimensions to return to a familiar section.

Notably section 48, where you can select a fresh direction or retrace your steps and try a more sensible answer.

Section 46

"Wrong!" exclaims the Wizard, staring at you with an appalled expression on his face. "How on earth did you get this far when you don't even know a simple thing like that?" He blinks, then a sheepish expression crosses his face. "Wait a minute—you're right! My silly mistake. You're quite right. Quite, quite right! As right as somebody with no left foot. Yes, well, you forget these things when you get to my age. Now, next question and this one is very, very difficult. Which of these three is associated with Jupiter—cabbage, beetroot, or garlic?"

Bad luck! Who remembers stuff like that? But you'd better give him an answer. If you think it's cabbage, go to 79. If you think it's beetroot, go to 109. If you think it's garlic, go to 90.

Section 47

"Sorry," says the Apothecary regretfully. "I fear they have outbid you."

Leaving you with the miserable options of fighting the Trolls at 72 or allowing yourself to be cooked and eaten, which you can try to forget at 13.

Well, now you've managed to get into the village, you'd better look around. You can work through trial and error if you like, but this is probably a good place to use your pendulum. However you work, select a number on the map and go off to see what you can find.

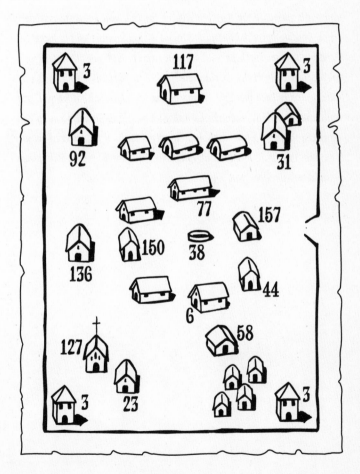

Section 49

"Call this a room? I've seen better accommodation in a rabbit hutch," you inform the Landlord, bopping him firmly on the nose.

"You'll be sorry you did that," he tells you.

And indeed you might. The Landlord has 22 Life Points, but before you grab your die for the first attack (which you get automatically since you've already bopped him) I should point out you aren't fighting to the death here. (No, you aren't. Not over the state of a room. You only fight to the death over important things.) If you manage to reduce his Life Points by 10, you can take it he will surrender at 118. However, the Landlord himself is under no such constraints, having been attacked unexpectedly by a crazed young Trainee Wizard. He will attempt to kill you if he possibly can. Should he succeed, you will sleep at 13.

Section 50

"No, no!" the Apothecary exclaims. "I tried that one and it doesn't work. My theory is that the clue is somehow related to the Wizard's Oracle. You know—the one you learned about in Lesson Eight. The Welsh Wizard's Oracle. Remember that one? I think perhaps each sentence of the clue might be the answer to a particular die roll so you need to work the Oracle backward, so to speak. Instead of rolling dice and looking up the answer, you look up the answer and find out what the dice roll was. Then if you put the two numbers together, you find the section you have to go to. That's my theory anyway. I didn't have time to test it out before you appeared, but that's what I think you should do. I could be wrong, of course."

Yes, he could be. What does the clue say again? "The friendship of somebody you know will affect this. You'll get help on this from somebody you don't know yet." And what were his notes? "Maybe just give up and go somewhere else entirely. Maybe combine the number of letters in the longest word with the number in the shortest word and go there. My pendulum says its 102, but I couldn't get that to work . . ."

If you just give up and go somewhere else entirely, I suppose that means returning to 48 and selecting a new destination. The longest word has eight letters and the shortest three, which combined would give you 83. His pendulum says 102 and it might be worth checking that just in case it works better for him than for you. Failing all else, maybe you should take up his suggestion about the Wizard's Oracle. There might be something in it.

Section 51

There is a distinct grinding noise as the sarcophagus moves a quarter of an inch, then stops. You wait expectantly, but nothing else happens.

"Well," says the Fiend, looking at you severely, "it seems you don't actually know the spell after all. Call yourself a Trainee Wizard? Call yourself an adventurer? Get back to 48 and don't come back here until you know exactly how many letters are in that spell!" With which he leaps back into his sarcophagus and pulls the lid shut after him.

Better take the Fiend's advice and continue your adventure at 48. Once you find out how many letters there really are in the anti-bear-baiting spell you can go directly to 82.

Section 52

You cough discreetly to attract the Apothecary's attention. "Listen," you whisper out of the side of your mouth, "my parents are multibillionaires and my personal allowance is enough to clear the national debt of several small countries. If you're prepared to let me go now, when I get back home I shall send you a dollar draft that will make you rich beyond your dreams."

A strange gurgling sound erupts from the Apothecary and his face turns bright red as if he was choking. After a moment you realize he is laughing.

All the same, he might go for it. Try an Absolutely Anything Roll. If it kills you, go to 13. If it succeeds, go to 156. If it fails, your only hope is to fight the Trolls at 72.

Section 53

There's lucky. You've found a little dagger somebody dropped. It's old and rusty and won't last more than three fights, but as long as it does last, you can add one point to any damage you score against monsters in a fight. Beside the dagger are three gold pieces, which might come in handy as well.

That's the good news. The bad news is you can't put off your decision where to go any longer.

If you want to investigate the glimmer of light, turn to 81. If you're gripped by lunacy and feel like risking the dark passage, go to 160. Use your pendulum to decide if you wish.

You press the curious symbol on the wall and at once there is a grinding noise behind the altar. You investigate to find a trap has opened in the floor of the church, revealing a flight of worn stone steps descending into darkness.

You hesitate for a moment before you notice a torch and tinderbox in a wall niche beside the first step. It takes you a little time to figure out the tinderbox, but being a bright young Trainee Wizard, you manage it eventually and the torch flares brightly.

Cautiously you step into the secret passage. The air grows damp and a little chill as you descend the steps. Despite your torch it is difficult to see where you are going, but eventually the stairs stop and enter a narrow passageway. You follow the passage for some two hundred yards before you reach an unlocked door which leads into a stone-lined chamber.

Shadows dance and flicker on the walls. At the far side of the chamber, on the edge of your vision, there seems to be a large stone sarcophagus. The place is silent as a tomb. Silent, that is, except for that peculiar coughing noise lions make on the African veldt.

So that's why the Priest called it the lion picture! What he really meant was it opened up a passage to a lion's den. Why on earth would he send you here when you told him you wanted to get to Carnegie Hall? Unless he saw through your cunning ruse and realized you actually wanted to get to the Wizards' Guild, of which he obviously disapproves deeply. But even then—

Look, do you really have time for this speculation when there is a large lion padding toward you out of the shadows? You can fight the brute to the death at **64** or try to tame it at **105**.

Carefully checking to make sure your head is still on its shoulders, you look around the grisly relics in the room and discover the Headman preserved the shrunken heads using liberal doses of healing potion. There's enough of it in a pot on the sideboard to make you three potions, each one capable of restoring a double dice roll of Life Points. Beside the pot there is a most intriguing scrap of paper, apparently the remains of a letter the Headman received some time. The letterhead is that of the Wizards' Guild!

Unfortunately most of the letter has been destroyed, including the return address, but what does remain is the number 5.

Which isn't a lot of good to anybody. Could mean fifty something or five hundred and something or something and five—you just wouldn't know. But at least you now have three healing potions. Take them with you to 48 where you can select a new destination, hopefully a bit safer than this last one.

Section 56

The little man stares at you for a long moment then slowly shakes his head. "Afraid not," he says dolefully. Then he brightens, "Tell you what: You look like a very nice young person, just the sort we'd welcome in the Wizards' Guild. Why don't you have another try? You know the Wizard's Wing handle isn't red now, so is it yellow, blue, or olive, citrine, russet and black?"

If you think it's yellow, go to 39. If you'd prefer blue, go to 25. Or give the olive, citrine, etc., answer at 71.

With a sigh of utter greed, you leap into the treasury and begin to fill your pockets.

How much cash you collect depends how well you do in your next few dice rolls. Make ten—yes, ten—double dice rolls and add the results together. That's how much gold there is in the treasury. You can take it all or just part of it, depending on your whim. If you take more than fifty gold pieces, go to 116. If you take less, go to 122.

Section 58

That's more like it. This humble cottage is obviously the home of a Wizard—it's floating six inches off the ground! You raise your hand to knock at the front door, but it opens before you can do so. Standing in the threshold is an elderly man with a long gray beard dressed in flowing robes (which is a peculiar way to dress a long gray beard.) He glares at you suspiciously. "Well, the Wizard's Oracle (advanced version) warned me somebody would be knocking in the next five seconds with my Fire Wand. Did you bring it?"

"Bring it?" you repeat stupidly, taken aback by the accuracy of his prediction and wondering how you can get hold of the advanced version of the Wizard's Oracle.

"The Wand, you blithering idiot! The Fire Wand!"

Well, have you brought him his Fire Wand? If you have, give it to him at 114. No use pretending if you haven't—your only hope is to get back to 48 and select another destination.

"Wrong!" roars the mighty figure before you. "Now you *must* take my advice, for that is the Wizardly law!"

So saying, he waves one huge hand and at once you are taken up and spun around in a vortex of magical enemies. For a moment you feel yourself flying through the stars and galaxies of deep space before you pass painfully through a multiplicity of dimensions to return to a familiar section.

*Notably section **48** where you can select a fresh direction or retrace your steps and try a more sensible answer.*

Section 60

"There you are, my good man," you say grandly. "Take this gold in full and complete payment and keep this rusty old washer I found for yourself."

"Thank you, kindly little Wizard," he grovels, bowing, scraping and tugging his forelock. "Much obliged, I'm sure. Thankee. Thankee." He bites the washer to make sure it's genuine and turns a little green from the lead content. "This way, young rich, handsome, dominant, alpha-type person of means and substance."

With which he steps to one side, thus allowing you to proceed to **48**.

"Walk this way, sir," says the Landlord, limping toward a narrow staircase.

You limp after him, wondering why he wants you to walk that way, and together you climb to an attic room with a sloping floor and low ceiling. There is a pile of smelly straw in one corner.

"Is this it?" you ask in amazement.

"No refunds," says the Landlord quickly.

This clown is trying it on. If you're feeling chicken, you can smile ingratiatingly, thank him for the room, and try to get a night's sleep at 159. Alternatively, you can try beating him to a pulp at 49.

Section 62

Three minutes after you take off, the Pilot reports engine trouble. Two minutes after that, the rotor blades catch fire. Following which the fuel tank explodes, the Pilot bails out but you grab the controls and somehow manage to nurse the flaming machine all the way to the island.

Which you'll find at 28.

She stares at you for a moment, then sniffs. "Can't say I'm impressed by that," she says. "Not impressed at all. Are you impressed, Harold?"

The Cat shakes his head. "Singularly unimpressed," he says.

You wait for a moment, then ask, "Does this mean you're not going to tell me how to get to the Wizards' Guild?"

She sniffs again. "That's exactly what it means. I'd suggest you do a little revision of your Wizardry lessons before you come back here again. Meanwhile, Harold and I believe you should return to 48 and seek another destination since there is nothing for you here."

You heard the lady. Off you go to Section 48.

Section 64

"Eeeeaaaaaaaah!" you cry, enunciating the age-old Wizard War Cry, as you hurl yourself upon the savage beast.

Sometimes I think you ought to be committed. But you've done it now, so there's no turning back. The savage beast in question has a massive 29 Life Points and an extra two points fang-and-claw damage in every roll scored against you. If you manage to kill the brute, which frankly I feel highly unlikely, you can go to 167. If not, then claw your way to 13.

You hurl yourself forward like a scalded cheetah. The building hurls itself backward at much the same speed.

That didn't help, did it? Try moving toward it more slowly at 89, or backing away from it at 119, or retrace your steps to 138 and see if you can approach it from a different direction.

Section 66

Look out! Look out! The cliff face is crumbling! You're losing your grip! You're beginning to fall!

You've caught a daisy! You're hanging by a daisy! The daisy is pulling out by the roots! You're falling!

You're plunging at a fierce rate to a broken, mangled, splatted ending on the jagged rocks below! You're screaming!

"Ahhhhhhhhhhhhhhhhhhhhhhhhhhhhhhhhhhhhhhhhhhhhh-hhhhhhhhhhhh!"

You're—wait a minute, you've stopped falling and you're still intact. More or less. You're on a narrow ledge, your heart beating furiously. Below you, the cliff face has fallen away so there is no possibility whatsoever of climbing down. But to your right there is the entrance to a narrow tunnel that bores at an acute angle into the cliff.

You can stay on the ledge until you starve to death, in which case go to 13. Or you can risk the tunnel at 133.

"My dear Fiend," you begin in your most ingratiating manner. "The fame of your poetry has spread far and wide while the verse itself brings joy and happiness to—"

But the Poetic Fiend isn't listening. He's looking past you to the tawny body on the floor of the chamber. "You've killed Fido!" he screams. "You've killed my pet lion!"

With which he leaps on you and rips your throat out.

Leaving you speechless at 13, which might teach you to be a bit kinder to animals.

Section 68

The winged creature looks at you grumpily. "Yes, well, that's right as a matter of fact, so I have to let you go ahead—"

"And me," puts in the Apothecary.

"—And you," nods the Archangel. "Although I still say you shouldn't be doing this at all." With which he folds his wings and disappears into his own dimension of the universe.

"Odd creatures," remarks the Apothecary as you walk together through an archway into the mouth of a labyrinthine maze.

You stop. "What's this?" you ask suspiciously.

"Just one of the little ordeals I mentioned," says the Apothecary. "There are ten exits from this maze. One of them takes you to the Wizards' Guild. One of them takes you to your doom. I'm afraid the other eight all eventually lead back to section 48. The idea is that you use your pendulum to select the right path. It's actually not much of an ordeal—there's only one chance in ten of your getting killed."

Doesn't sound like great odds to me, but if you want to risk it, that's your choice. Here are the paths that lead to the ten maze exits—26, 33, 43, 74, 93, 121, 129, 135, 155, 169. Get your pendulum into gear and let's see if you get out of this one with your whole skin.

Section 69

"Thought I told you to clear orf," mutters the Guard as he emerges from the rickety tower. "Now I'll have to beat you to a pulp and feed the residue to the Village Well Monster."

"You and whose army?" you ask him cleverly.

"Oooooh, like I never heard that one before. Come on, let's get this over with so I can go back up to keep a lookout for real trouble."

"You've got real trouble here," you tell him, advancing menacingly.

But despite the brave words, it may be you who's in real trouble. The Guard has 18 Life Points, which isn't all that high (high enough, though), but you can now see for the first time that he's armed. It may be only a pitchfork—the military tradition in this village leaves much to be desired—but it still adds 2 to every damage roll he scores against you. What's more, if he manages to score 6 twice running, you're dead however many Life Points you happen to have left.

Should the Guard kill you, which I must say sounds exceedingly likely, go to 13. Should you kill him, you can search the corpse at 85.

Section 70

Uh-oh, something not quite right here. As you walk into the living room of the Village Headman's home, you find every shelf and cupboard is jam-packed with shrunken heads.

He catches your startled expression. "It's my hobby," he tells you. "That's why they call me the Village Headman. Now if you'll just step over to the guillotine, I can add yours to my collection."

*Looks like you've just found yourself a picturesque psycho. It's fight or flight time. If you decide discretion is the better part of valor and want to run for it, you'll need an **Absolutely Anything Roll** which, if it doesn't kill you, will allow you to return to 48. Alternatively, of course, you can fight for your life. The Headman comes equipped with 21 Life Points and will guillotine you instantly if he manages to roll two consecutive 6s during the fight. If you win, you can stagger off to 55. If not, regrow your head at 13.*

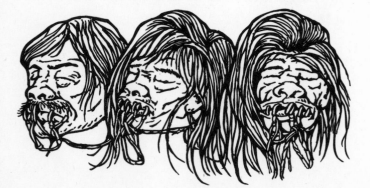

The little man stares at you for a long moment then slowly shakes his head. "Afraid not," he says dolefully. Then he brightens, "Tell you what. You look like a very nice young person, just the sort we'd welcome in the Wizards' Guild. Why don't you have another try? You know the Wizard's Wing handle isn't olive, citrine, russet, and black now, so is it yellow, red, or blue?"

If you think it's yellow, go to 39. If you'd prefer red, go to 56. Or give the blue answer at 25.

Section 72

"Have at you!" you roar suddenly. "Think I'm going to stand here and let you eat me? No indeed, I am not. I shall fight you on the beaches. I shall fight you in the hills. I shall fight you in the fields and in the streets. I shall never—"

Wait a minute! Wait a minute! There are twenty-eight Trolls, not to mention the Apothecary with his Fire Wand. It's utter and complete suicide to fight them all. Are you quite sure you don't have money you could use to bribe him at 149? Or failing that, can't you promise him a reward at 52? If you insist on fighting, they're all ready and waiting for you at 87.

Three hundred yards down the road you are set upon by Robin Hood and his Merrie Men who are convinced despite all your protestations that you are the Sheriff of Nottingham. Contrary to his PR image, Robin is not the gentleman robber we have all been led to believe, but the sort of villain who makes any monster look like an Episcopalian vicar. His Merrie Men are even worse, as you might guess from a bunch of smelly, unwashed, illiterates who spell "merry" the way they do. Thus you are tied to a tree with your bootlaces and used for target practice.

Unfortunately, despite their many failings, this lot are all excellent archers.

Once they've finished turning you into a pin-cushion, you can pull the arrows out at 13. And do try to be more careful with the Pyramid Oracle in future.

Section 74

You twist and turn, turn and twist, return and retwist, coil, wriggle, back up, get confused, unconfuse yourself, snake about a bit, and finally . . .

Emerge at 139. Looks promising. You're not dead (yet) and you're definitely not back at 48.

Section 75

"Wrong!" exclaims the Wizard, staring at you with an appalled expression on his face. "How on earth did you get this far when you don't even know a simple thing like that?"

So saying, he makes a mystic gesture and magically transports you to—

To where? Roll one die. Score 1 or 2 and continue your adventure from 77. Score 3 or 4 and continue it from 92. Score 5 or 6 and continue it from 127. And if you want my advice, I'd look up the answer to that question before I got back here again.

Section 76

Some nice stuff here, but most of it is troll size and hence no good to you at all. But there is a sword that will give you three extra damage points in any roll you make against monsters in a fight and a breastplate that will deduct the same number of points from any roll made against you.

Now, if you haven't already done so, you can loot their treasury at 57, take the underpass at 97, follow the path he says leads to the Wizards' Guild at 106, or explore the tunnel you shouldn't go into under any circumstances whatsoever at 151.

Boy, does that smell good! Your nose tells you where you are even before you walk through the door. It's a pie shop! Game pies, steak pies, pigeon pies, fish pies, oyster pies, eel pies, apple pies, blueberry pies, deep-dish pies, lattice pies, plus a whole selection of tarts—lemon, bakewell, treacle, you name it.

"Pies . . . mmm, pies . . . arrragh," you drool in a passable imitation of a starved castaway.

"All home baked," says the plump, rosy-cheeked motherly woman behind the counter. "And all one price—a silver piece each."

I'd strongly suggest you buy one if you can afford it. Never know where the next meal's coming from on the Wizard's Adventure. But whether you buy a pie or not, you should certainly get back to 48 and select another destination as quickly as possible—you're drooling so much you're making a mess on the floor.

Section 78

As you approach the helicopter pad, you notice three choppers waiting on the tarmac, doors open and engines ticking over. They look like they've been painted by an American patriot (or possibly a British patriot) since one is red, one is white, and one is blue.

"Which of you is going to the island?" you call, but the Pilots can't hear you over the sound of their engines.

Looks like you're going to have to make another pendulum choice. You can board the red chopper at 37, the white at 62, or the blue at 158.

"Wrong!" exclaims the Wizard, staring at you with an appalled expression on his face. "How on earth did you get this far when you don't even know a simple thing like that?"

So saying, he makes a mystic gesture and magically transports you to—

To where? Roll one die. Score 1 or 2 and continue your adventure from 77. Score 3 or 4 and continue it from 92. Score 5 or 6 and continue it from 127. And if you want my advice, I'd look up the answer to that question before I got back here again.

Section 80

"Well done!" exclaims the Apothecary. "If you'll kindly hand over every gold piece you possess, I shall conduct you directly to 48 where you can select another destination, although you will probably wish to avoid meeting me again."

Too right! Go to 48 and select another destination, avoiding all apothecaries.

Section 81

Good grief, you've found your way out of the cave! That glimmer of light was the entrance! How easy was that? Now all you have to do is find a path to the nearest town, make a few inquiries about the Wizards' Guild, and—

Uh-oh, problems. As you reach the cave's mouth, you discover it actually opens out onto a sheer cliff face with a drop of several hundred feet straight down. Across some heavily forested countryside you can see the church spires of a bustling town, but reaching it from here could be very difficult.

All the same, you could try climbing down the cliff at 27. Risky, but it's your decision. Alternatively, you can retrace your steps to 1 and pick another option there. Use your pendulum to help you decide.

Section 82

As you stand nervously waiting to be fanged, the Fiend bursts into a patter of applause, slightly muffled by his white gloves. "Exquisite!" he exclaims. "Such sensitivity! Such creativity! Such taste! Such intelligence! An epic worthy of the Bard of Avon, a poem to put Shelley to shame! Well done! Well done!"

You blink. "Does this mean you'll help me find my way to the Wizards' Guild?" you ask.

"Of course, of course. Clearly you are exactly the type of young person the Guild needs. There is a tunnel underneath my sarcophagus that leads you directly to the doorway of the Guild where you will undergo your final tests. But I'm certain someone with your dedication to Wizardry will pass them easily." He steps to one side and gestures grandly toward his sarcophagus.

"How do I move it to get at the secret tunnel?" you ask.

"Simplicity itself," exclaims the Poetic Fiend grandly. "Simply tell me how many letters there are in the anti-bear-baiting spell."

Oh dear. If you think there are seven letters in the spell, go to 42. If you think there are nine letters in the spell, go to 51. If you think there are eleven letters in the spell, go to 19. If you haven't a bull's notion how many letters there are in the spell, get yourself back to 48 and continue to adventure until you find out.

"No, no!" the Apothecary exclaims. "I tried that one and it doesn't work. My theory is that the clue is somehow related to the Wizard's Oracle. You know—the one you learned about in Lesson Eight. Not the Pyramid Oracle—the Wizard's Oracle. The Welsh Wizard's Oracle. Remember that one? The one you work with dice. I think perhaps each sentence of the clue might be the answer to a particular die roll so you need to work the Oracle backward, so to speak. Instead of rolling dice and looking up the answer, you look up the answer and find out what the dice roll was. Then if you put the two numbers together, you find the section you have to go to. That's my theory anyway. I didn't have time to test it out before you appeared, but that's what I think you should do. I could be wrong, of course."

Yes, he could be. What does the clue say again? "The friendship of somebody you know will affect this. You'll get help on this from somebody you don't know yet." And what were his notes? "Maybe double the number of words, add ten, and go to that section? Maybe just give up and go somewhere else entirely. My pendulum says its 102, but I couldn't get that to work . . ."

*If you double the number of words and add ten, it'll take you to section **50**. If you just give up and go somewhere else entirely, I suppose that means returning to **48** and selecting a new destination. His pendulum says **102** and it might be worth checking that just in case it works better for him than for you. Failing all else, maybe you should take up his suggestion about the Wizard's Oracle. There might be something in it.*

Section 84

"Take that and that and that!" you scream, jumping up and down in a berserk rage. It's to little avail since the body of your opponent has dissolved into alchemical goo for some reason.

Leave behind the Fire Wand though, which means you now have an extra three points' damage in every throw against any opponent once you make your way back to 48 and select another destination.

You begin expertly to search the corpse, one of your more disgusting habits. There are two silver pieces in the pocket of his britches and a scrap of filthy parchment stuck down one sock. The parchment seems to have some sort of crude map drawn on it:

At the top of the map you can just make out the words "Wizard G" while near the middle somebody has written "Danger here." "Wizard G"? Surely that has to be the Wizards' Guild! If only you knew where the map referred to. Excitedly you turn it over in the hope there might be something on the back, but as you do so a heavy hand falls on your shoulder.

You turn to find you are surrounded by villagers armed with a variety of muskets, pitchforks, swords, bows, tanks, helicopter gunships, and intercontinental ballistic missiles.

"You killed a Guard!" exclaims the man with his hand on your shoulder.

"Indeed I did," you tell him easily. "He put up a good fight, but I and my trusty dice eventually got the better of him."

"But that's *murder!*" exclaims the villager appalled. "You don't think you can go around murdering people just because you're on the Wizard's Adventure, do you?"

"Well, I—" you begin.

But before you have a chance to explain, you are grabbed roughly and marched off to 143.

Section 86

"Wrong!" roars the mighty figure before you. "Now you *must* take my advice, for that is the Wizardly law!"

So saying, he waves one huge hand and at once you are taken up and spun around in a vortex of magical enemies. For a moment you feel yourself flying through the stars and galaxies of deep space before you pass painfully through a multiplicity of dimensions to return to a familiar section.

Notably section 48, where you can select a fresh direction or retrace your steps and try a more sensible answer.

Section 87

"—surrender!" you howl, completing the sentence.

"It's an option," says one Troll thoughtfully.

"Definitely an option," agrees another.

"Why don't we do that?" asks a third.

"I concur," nods a fourth.

"Very well," says the first Troll firmly. "We surrender."

"So do I," mutters the Apothecary sheepishly.

Not the most predictable result in the world, but it's happened. So what do you do now? The Trolls will take you on a tour of their island at 132. The Apothecary says he will show you the way off it at 126.

"No problem there," you say. "Piece of cake, actually. Every-body knows it's Mars, fourth planet from the Sun, nearest planet to Earth. Sometimes called the Red Planet. Romans named it their God of War. Has the largest volcano in the solar system. Yes, it's Mars. Definitely Mars. Final answer."

*At which point the Sphinx looks quite disappointed that she can't beat you to a pulp, tear you to pieces, decapitate you, jump up and down on the bits that are left, and send you off to 13. Instead, she stands aside grumpily and waves you on to **140**.*

Section 89

You move forward more slowly. The building recedes more slowly, but it still recedes.

You could run at it again, a bit faster this time, at 65. Or you could try backing away from it at 119. Or you could retrace your steps to 138 and see if you can approach it from a different direction.

Section 90

"Wrong!" exclaims the Wizard, staring at you with an appalled expression on his face. "How on earth did you get this far when you don't even know a simple thing like that?"

So saying, he makes a mystic gesture and magically transports you to—

To where? Roll one die. Score 1 or 2 and continue your adventure from 77. Score 3 or 4 and continue it from 92. Score 5 or 6 and continue it from 127. And if you want my advice, I'd look up the answer to that question before I got back here again.

Section 91

"Mutter-mutter financially embarrassed mutter-mutter," you mutter, "but I wonder if I might ask you something?"

"Ask away," the Landlord says expansively.

"I was wondering if you might possibly know the way to the Wizards' Guild?" you ask.

"I know it's well hidden," the Landlord tells you soberly. "And I know it's difficult to join. But as to its exact location . . ." He shrugs.

"Can you at least tell me if it's in this village?"

"Oh yes, it's in this village all right. I do know that. And there was a traveller in here just the other day—young person much like yourself—who mentioned that you reach it through the Crypt of the Fiend, wherever that might be. Sorry, but that's the most I can tell you."

Actually, it's not bad. Now you can get back to 48 and start searching for the Crypt of the Fiend.

Nice place. It's log-built, but a step or two up on your average holiday cabin. The grass around it has been nicely kept as well, which makes a big difference to a property I always think. You push through the little gate (ignoring the BEWARE OF THE SHEEP notice) walk up the narrow path to the front door. There's a notice there as well. It says VILLAGE HEADMAN. Bit of luck, that. If anybody can tell you where the Wizards' Guild might be it's surely the Village Headman. You knock firmly.

After a few moments the door is opened by a plump, open-faced man wearing brown britches and a green doublet. "Ah, a stranger to our humble village," he says heartily. "No doubt a weary traveller or enthusiastic young person embarked on the Wizard's Adventure. Come in! Come in!"

What a nice welcome. Might be a cup of coffee and a slice of apple pie in this if you play your cards right. You can accept the Village Headman's invitation at 70. But if you're feeling pressed for time, you can simply ask him where the Wizards' Guild might be by going to 141. You can even turn on your heel and walk right back to 48. Bit rude, but it's up to you.

Section 93

You twist and turn, turn and twist, return and retwist, coil, wriggle, back up, get confused, unconfuse yourself, snake about a bit and finally . . .

Emerge at 48. Sorry.

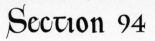

"Wrong!" exclaims the Wizard, staring at you with an appalled expression on his face. "How on earth did you get this far when you don't even know a simple thing like that?"

So saying, he makes a mystic gesture and magically transports you to—

To where? Roll one die. Score 1 or 2 and continue your adventure from 77. Score 3 or 4 and continue it from 92. Score 5 or 6 and continue it from 127. And if you want my advice, I'd look up the answer to that question before I got back here again.

Section 95

"By Jove, that's it!" exclaims the Apothecary as the section of bookshelves slides silently back to reveal the secret passage beyond. He smiles at you benignly. "All you have to do is follow the passage. There are one or two small ordeals, of course, but nothing a young Trainee Wizard of your caliber can't handle. And there may be a few simple questions when you reach the Guild, but you'll answer them easily. Well, glad to be of help and nice to meet you."

He stands to one side to let you enter the passage.

One or two small ordeals? Are you really sure you want to get into this? I mean it's not all that important to join the Wizards' Guild. Besides, there's probably some other, safer way. Why not slip back to 48 and pick another destination? But if you absolutely insist on entering the secret passage, you can do so at 131.

The passageway winds downward in a most alarming fashion, but eventually the darkness gives way to gloom, then a dusky light. Ahead you can see a brighter light and when you reach it you step out at last into bright sunshine. With a deep sigh of heartfelt relief, you look around.

You are standing at the bottom of a cliff face. High above you can see the entrance to the cave where you started this adventure. Around you is dense woodland and a narrow pathway directly ahead winds so drunkenly that you quickly lose your sense of direction. But after walking for almost fifteen minutes, you reach a crossroads. The four arms of the signpost read:

Back The Way You Came ➤ **5**.

Wizards' Guild ➤ **147**.

How About This Way? ➤ **123**.

Is This Right? ➤ **73**.

How about that? You've hardly started your adventure and already you've found the road to the Wizards' Guild. It's almost too easy, but the other directions aren't very helpful. So troll on off to 147 without delay . . . unless you want to make with a mysterious smile and check out those directions in a Wizardly way.

Still seems too good to be true, but this route really does take you off the island with no problems whatsoever, no dangers, no fights, no trickery.

How about that? It leads you safely all the way to 48.

Section 98

He stares at you with a pained expression. "This is devastating," he says. "I really thought you were home and dry. That's the wrong answer! I can't believe it. You've come so far. Just this one final hurdle and suddenly you're goosed. Done for. Relegated to the ranks of the terminally ordinary. Why on earth didn't you sneakily look up the answer before you gave it? It's there in the lesson about Wizard Space. I can't let you come this far and dump you right back at the beginning. Tell you what: You do a bit of revision on the Wizard Space lesson and you can restart your adventure with all your Life Points, golden keys, and other stuff absolutely intact at 48. Just work your way from there and get it right next time!"

You heard what the man said. Go to Wizard Space, then 48.

"How dare you pull the wool over my eyes!" you scream in an unusually old-fashioned manner. "For that you die—at least in this virtual world of the Wizard's Adventure."

"Easier said than done," grins the Apothecary.

Never a truer word spoken. Despite his unprepossessing appearance, this clown has no fewer than 30 Life Points due to all the vitamins he takes. Furthermore, that Fire Wand gives him an extra three points of damage in every throw against you. If he wins the fight, proceed, as always, to 13. If you come out on top, it would be a good idea to go to 84.

Section 100

She stares at you for a moment, then sniffs. "Must say I'm impressed by that," she says. "Quite impressed. Are you impressed, Harold?"

The Cat nods his head. "Singularly impressed," he says.

You wait for a moment, then ask, "Does this mean you're not going to tell me how to get to the Wizards' Guild?"

She sniffs again. "That's exactly what it means. Or almost exactly. I mean, I can't send you there directly—that would never do. But I can put you on the right track. I suggest you pray."

You wait. After a long moment it becomes clear she's not about to say anything else. "Is that it?" you ask in astonishment.

"That's it," she says, "and a very good clue it is."

Harold and she both stare at you with that insufferably smug expression of people who know more than you do.

Well, apart from staring back, the only thing you can do now is get back to 48 and pick another destination.

"Look, can't we talk this over?" you ask reasonably. "I mean, there's absolutely no need for—"

He waves a languid hand. "In verse, my dear young person, in verse! I am far too sensitive and artistic to converse in any other manner. If you are capable to introducing yourself in a short poem, I shall consider helping you out. Otherwise I shall compose a memorial ode, then fang you in the throat."

Jeepers, what are you going to do now? Tell you what—I'll leave you a little space on this page . . .

See if you can manage to write three or four rhyming lines about yourself in the space. Hopefully it has to be better than the rubbish he spouts. When you've finished, turn to 82 to find out what he thinks of it.

_____

_____

_____

_____

Section 102

"No, no!" the Apothecary exclaims. "I tried that one and it doesn't work. My theory is that the clue is somehow related to the Wizard's Oracle. You know—the one you learned about in Lesson Eight. Not the Pyramid Oracle—the Wizard's Oracle. The Welsh Wizard's Oracle. Remember that one? The one you work with dice. I think perhaps each sentence of the clue might be the answer to a particular die roll so you need to work the Oracle backward, so to speak. Instead of rolling dice and looking up the answer, you look up the answer and find out what the dice roll was. Then if you put the two numbers together, you find the section you have to go to. That's my theory anyway. I didn't have time to test it out before you appeared, but that's what I think you should do. I could be wrong, of course."

Yes, he could be. What does the clue say again? "The friendship of somebody you know will affect this. You'll get help on this from somebody you don't know yet." *And what were the relevant parts of his notes?* "Maybe double the number of words, add ten, and go to that section? Maybe just give up and go somewhere else entirely. Maybe combine the number of letters in the longest word with the number in the shortest word and go there,"

If you double the number of words and add ten, it'll take you to section 50. If you just give up and go somewhere else entirely, I suppose that means returning to 48 and selecting a new destination. The longest word has eight letters and the shortest three, which combined would give you 83. Failing all else, maybe you should take up his suggestion about the Wizard's Oracle. There might be something in it.

"All right," you say. "You have an honest face, albeit a mournful and rather ugly one. I think I believe you, so will you please break the hypnotic trance that makes me believe the Guild is just over there?"

"Sure thing," he says. "But where would you like to wake up? I can give you the choice of 110, 128, or 134. None of them will kill you, but some are a little better than others."

Looks like it might be pendulum time again. Take your pick between 110, 128, and 134. And good luck.

Section 104

"Eight gold pieces? Are you out of your mind?" you exclaim. "I wouldn't pay a brass farthing to a smelly, ugly, dimwitted, little tort-feasor like you. I suspect your mother was a retarded weasel and your father was a goat. And they both must be embarrassed at how their son turned out. I flip the bird and blow a raspberry to indicate my contempt of you."

With these courageous taunts, you hurl yourself upon him.

I'm not sure this is necessarily such a good idea. The yokel has 20 Life Points and that pitchfork's just been sharpened so it will enable him to do an additional three points of damage on every die roll he makes against you. If you survive this fight, you'll find a healing potion worth a double die roll of Life Points in his back pocket, after which you can step over the body and proceed to 48. If you lose the fight, you get nothing for your pains (which will be considerable by then) except a quick trip to 13.

"Here kitty, kitty," you call out enticingly. "Here nice kitty-cat . . . would you like some milk? Saucer of cream? A live zebra?"

The savage brute pads toward you.

"Come on, puss-puss, let's be friends."

The savage brute reaches you, opens its gigantic mouth, and licks your outstretched hand with an extremely rough tongue. Then it starts to purr. To your astonishment it rolls over on its back to have its tummy tickled.

Well, I wouldn't have given a wooden nickel for your chances of that result. But it certainly seems as if you've successfully tamed the lion. Turn swiftly to 152 to find out what happens next!

Section 106

They told the truth! There it is! After no more than half a mile, you're actually in sight of the Wizards' Guild! It's housed in a beautiful old mansion set in its own grounds with the words *Wizards' Guild* floating above it etched in fire. You start to run toward it, but curiously it seems to recede.

You stop, wondering what to do next.

Well, you could run at it again, a bit faster this time, at 65. Or try moving toward it more slowly at 89, see if that makes any difference. Or you could try backing away from it at 119. Or you could retrace your steps to 138 and see if you can approach it from a different direction. Have I thought of everything? Good. Make your choice.

Carefully stepping over the open sewer and avoiding the bubbling cauldron, you enter the grotty cottage . . . and immediately discover it's far larger on the inside than the outside. Cleaner, too, and delightfully furnished in the modern style with emphasis on strip lighting, glass, and brushed chrome. There are several comfortable armchairs in a bright, tastefully carpeted living room and while there is a Witch's Cat, it's rather a handsome animal that smiles and waves in a friendly, welcoming fashion as you enter.

The wizened old Crone straightens up and her hump disappears. She reaches up to her head like an alien in a sci-fi movie and carefully peels off the mask that conceals a beautiful face with delicate features and a torrent of shining auburn hair.

"That's better," she grins at you.

"But you're—you're—" you stammer.

"Yes, I am, aren't I?" she agrees. "I've always found it amusing to play up to people's image of a Witch. You know —ugly old crone, cauldron, broomstick, all that Medieval nonsense. Actually, we Witches are quite civilized these days. As you know, of course, since I gather you're a Trainee Wizard."

"That's quite true," you tell her. "And, of course, I wasn't fooled for a minute."

"So you'll join me for lunch? I was thinking of a dozen oysters, some caviar, salmon hollandaise, asparagus, minted new potatoes, and a bottle of the '85 Pouilly Fumé. With a double chocolate torte to follow, of course."

"With cream," adds her Cat.

"Yes," you tell her, swaying at the thought.

As you finish this truly magnificent meal, you burp slightly and broach the subject that concerns you most deeply. "I don't suppose you know where I might find the Wizards' Guild?" you ask.

"Yes, of course I do," she tells you promptly, "but since you're on the Wizard's Adventure, I'm only allowed to give you a hint. And even then only if you can answer an important question."

"What's the question?" you ask quickly.

"The question is this," says the Witch. "Which direction would you go to find Air?"

Well, no use sitting there looking at her with your mouth open. A Wizard should be able to answer a simple question like that easy peasy. If you think Air is North, go to 166. If you think it's South, go to 130. If you think it's East, go to 100. If you think it's West, go to 2. If you think you'll find Air in any direction, go to 63.

Section 108

You follow the tunnel until you find it completely blocked by a cave-in.

What a bummer! But at least you weren't underneath when it happened. For now, though, all you can do is retrace your steps and climb aboard the ferry at 165, swim using the scuba gear at 146, or board a chopper at 78.

Section 109

"Wrong!" exclaims the Wizard. "No—right! Yes, that's it. Got it in one! By Jove, you know your stuff. Just one more test—three's the charm, of course—and I can give you the key. Now, what is it I have to ask you . . . ?"

"Is that the test?" you ask.

"Is what the test?"

"Telling you what it is you have to ask me. Because if it is, you could ask me who I am—I usually get 75 percent in that. Or you could ask—"

The Wizard draws himself up to his full height. "I could ask you to take this whole business a little more seriously," he says with dignity. "Of course that wasn't the test. That was just my brain decaying slightly. Your third and final question is actually this—and think before you answer because it's tricky—when does a circle actually become a magic circle? When you draw it completely? When you imagine you've drawn it? Or when you fortify it with symbols and words of power?"

Tricky indeed—you're going to have to go to first principles on that one. If you think completing the circle makes the magic, go to 98. If you believe imagining a circle makes it magic, go to 9. If you think fortifying a circle makes it magic, turn to 168.

Section 110

You sit up with a jerk (who shall remain nameless) and look around you. To your absolute astonishment, the Wizards' Guild has disappeared, as has the mournful Wizard and, indeed, the entire island.

Leaving you standing gormlessly at 127.

Section 111

"No problem there," you say. "Piece of cake, actually. Everybody knows it's the Sun, not precisely a planet, more of a star really. Biggest body in the solar system, everything orbits around it, nice and warm in summer but you wouldn't want to live there. Yes, it's the Sun. Definitely the Sun. Final answer."

At which point the Sphinx beats you to a pulp, tears you to pieces, decapitates you, jumps up and down on the bits that are left, and sends you off to 13.

The passageway is extremely deceptive in that it twists, turns, and winds for far longer than you would have imagined. By the time you've trudged for a good ten minutes you're beginning to wonder if the Fiend might not have been playing some sort of ghastly joke on you.

But then suddenly you turn a corner and there it is—an iron-studded oakwood doorway above which, carved in stone, appears the legend "Wizards' Guild."

A cheerful, bespectacled, shaven-headed Wizard bustles forward to meet you. "Well done, well done, you found us!" he exclaims. "I do hope the Adventure wasn't too much of a burden. Now, just a few final questions before I give you the key. Just to make sure you really do know your Wizardry. First, how many lines are there in the Square of Mars—five, six or seven?"

If you think it's five, go to 46. Six, turn to 75. Or seven, get to 94.

Section 113

That was some punch-up! Lucky you came out of it in one piece (more or less). Now comes the nice bit—you can open the copper-bound chest.

Roll two dice. The score tells you how many gold pieces are in the chest. Also in there is a silver breastplate you can wear under your Wizard's robe, which deducts two points from any damage scored against you if you get into any more fights. However, a score of 12 means the chest was booby-trapped and you've lost a further 12 Life Points. If this kills you, go to 13. If not, the only way out of this cavern is back to 5.

"There you go, good sir," you say cheerfully, handing across the Wand. "Looks in excellent condition and my pleasure, sir—my absolute pleasure—to deliver it to you."

As he examines it closely, touching the end to the tip of his tongue suspiciously and biting the shaft a few times to test its strength, you give a depreciating cough. "Forgive me mentioning it, Your Wizardness, but I am a young Trainee Wizard (Third Degree) with ambitions to become as great—not to mention handsome—as your good self one day and to that end I was wondering if your gratitude for the delivery of the Wand might extend to your telling me where I might find the Wizards' Guild?"

"'Fraid not," says the Wizard, stowing the Wand away in his robes. "They expelled me last week and moved the whole place out of pique. There's one other member in the village, I believe, but her name escapes me. What I can do, however, is give you these—"

So saying he hands you a small green bottle of foul-smelling liquid and a golden key.

Small and foul-smelling it might be, but that bottle contains enough healing potion to restore a double dice roll of Life Points. No idea what the golden key is for, but you might as well hold on to it as you return to 48 and select another destination.

Section 115

"Think I'm afraid of you, you big bully?" you scream, hurling yourself on the gigantic figure. "I'll dice you to a pulp!"

A pained expression crosses the features of the gigantic figure, which twitches a pinkie (the left one) and sends you direct to 13.

Did you hear that? Direct to 13. That'll teach you to attack an Archangel.

Section 116

You are so loaded down with gold you are unable to defend yourself when the Chief Troll mounts a surprise attack and hacks you to 15,377 tiny pieces.

Which you can carefully reassemble at 13.

Section 117

This used to be quite a nice house, but that was before most of it fell down. What's left is a crumbling ruin of its former grandeur with broken windows and missing doors.

Odd thing is, there's a light inside.

Bit spooky, that. A light in a ruined manor? Could be anything—ghosts, spirits, nasty smelly old guys cooking their boots. Might be best if you went quietly back to 48 to select another destination. But if you absolutely positively definitely can't resist the compulsion to explore the ruin with its eerie light, you can do so at 11.

Section 118

"Enough! Enough!" the Landlord cries. "I surrender! I apologize! I refund your money! I find you somewhere much better to sleep! I throw in breakfast! I send you cards on your birthday and at Christmas! Please, please don't batter me with your dice any more!"

With which he leads you to a stateroom complete with four-poster bed and bathroom en suite where you spend a peaceful night and enjoy breakfast in bed the following morning.

Worth making a fuss. Don't forget he's refunded your money, so you add that back in to your total gold. Now, you can go off well-fed and refreshed to 48 to pick another destination.

Section 119

As you back away, the building moves forward, but since it moves forward at the same rate as you back away, the net result is that things stay pretty much the same.

Irritating. You could run at it again, a bit faster this time, at **65**. *Or try moving toward it more slowly at* **89**. *Or you could retrace your steps to* **138** *and see if you can approach it from a different direction.*

Section 120

A faint heart never won the Wizard's Adventure and, besides, those notices look pretty old. Might even be a practical joke—you can never tell with country humor. But whether obsolete or just plain nonsense, you ignore them with a vengeance as you approach the well.

A brass plaque screwed to the woodwork of the well reads:

Wishes must be made aloud and in rhyme if possible.
Thank you.

So you were right! It really is a wishing well! Not that you believe in wishing wells, of course, but no harm in trying this one out just in case. You never know, do you? Now you've started training as a Wizard, anything could happen. So after a moment's creative thought, you compose the following wish:

I wish, I wish, but not in vain
To find the Wizards' Guild again.

The "again" bit doesn't make a lot of sense since you haven't found the Wizards' Guild *before*, but at least it rhymes, which is what the plaque suggested. You go over it a few times in your head to make sure you have it word perfect, then lean over the opening of the well and chant it aloud:

I wish, I wish, but not in vain
To find the Wizards' Guild again.

At once a tentacle snakes up from the gloom of the well shaft, wraps itself around your throat, and drags you in.

Good grief, you've been grabbed by the Well Monster! No wonder there were warning notices. But no time for regrets—you've got a fight on your hands; and a big one. The Well Monster has 27 Life Points and a very nasty disposition. Worse still, it loves Trainee Wizards. (Which is to say it finds them delicious.) If the Monster wins the fight, it will eat all your edible bits and spit the bones to **13**. *In the unlikely event that you defeat the Monster, you can make your way to* **162**.

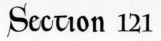

You twist and turn, turn and twist, return and retwist, coil, wriggle, back up, get confused, unconfuse yourself, snake about a bit, and finally . . .

Emerge at 48. Sorry.

Section 122

"That's enough for me!" you remark cheerfully. "Us Trainee Wizards are more interested in magical and spiritual pursuits than money."

Ah, would that it were true! But be that as it may, you can now equip yourself at their armory at 76, take the underpass at 97, follow the path he says leads to the Wizards' Guild at 106, or explore the tunnel you shouldn't go into under any circumstances whatsoever at 151.

Section 123

Three hundred yards along, the road narrows. Around you, birds stop singing and the small rustling sounds of nature grind to a halt. The sky grows overcast in a threatening, gothic fashion. The silence is palpable. It is the silence of a tomb.

Look, are you sure you want to keep going this way? I mean, you could always go back to 96 and pick another option. In fact, I can save you the trouble of going back. The options were: Back The Way You Came ➤ 96; Wizards' Guild ➤ 147; How About This Way? ➤ 123; Is This Right? ➤ 73. Well, you can obviously forget about "Back The Way You Came," which just puts you in an endless loop. And "How About This Way" is the road you're on now. But wouldn't you be at all interested in "Wizards' Guild" at 147 or "Is This Right?" at 73? It's your choice, of course, but it really is getting very creepy here. What does your pendulum advise? Maybe you should just forget the whole Wizards' Guild thing altogether— far too dangerous for somebody your age. Anyway, meditate on your choices and decide what you want to do.

(If you really want to keep on this road, go to 154.)

Section 124

"You realize I'm only doing this under protest," you mutter weakly.

"Shut up and prepare to be eaten," grunts the Apothecary.

You follow him meekly to the dark tower where you are met by a large group of Trolls, who stare at you hungrily.

"This young person is fully organic and guaranteed absolutely delicious!" announces the Apothecary. "Now, let's have my money and you can get on with your next meal."

Wait a minute. If all this clown cares about is money, maybe you can outbid the Trolls. If you have any gold with you, you can try this at 149. Even if you haven't, you could always try promising him money later at 52. Failing that, I suppose you could always try fighting the Trolls—even though there are rather a lot of them—at 72.

Section 125

"Take that and that and that and that!" you cry, hurling yourself upon him in a flurry of dice rolls.

"Help!" yells your helpless victim, who turns out not to be helpless after all since forty-eight of his fellow golfers appear instantly in response to his call.

"Leave our Captain alone!" they roar in unison.

After which they beat you up to the tune of a single die roll of Life Points (if this kills you, go to 13) after which they frog-march you from their club and hurl you facedown into section 48.

Section 126

He does, too, much to your surprise.

Just shows you can't even trust the baddies to be bad all the time. He waves goodbye to you at 48.

It's the village church. Might have guessed that from the map. Not very big, but then it's not a very big village. Nice example of High Medieval architecture, though. Stone built, very solid. The stained glass windows are a later addition obviously.

The iron-studded oakwood door is closed, but probably not locked. In any case it opens as you walk toward it. A Priest looks at you stern-facedly. "I hope you're not here to cause trouble," he tells you sternly. "I hope you're not one of those ghastly Trainee Wizards!"

"Perish the thought," you lie through your teeth. "Wizard? Me? Pah! Yugh! Puke!"

"Glad to hear it," says the Priest, "but you'll appreciate that since I deal with sinners in my professional capacity, I am naturally a little cynical and suspicious. Are you prepared to say a little prayer with me? If you're one of those ghastly Trainee Wizards, the prayer I have in mind will set your feet on fire and cause your brain to explode. In the circumstances, I'd prefer we said it out here in the open. I hate having to clean up afterward."

Well, are you going to risk a prayer that will set your feet on fire and cause your brain to explode? If so, take a deep breath and proceed to 7. If not, you can always back slowly to 48 and select another destination.

You sit up with a jerk and look around you. To your absolute astonishment, the Wizards' Guild has disappeared, as has the mournful Wizard and, indeed, the entire island.

Leaving you standing gormlessly at 150.

Section 129

You twist and turn, turn and twist, return and retwist, coil, wriggle, back up, get confused, unconfuse yourself, snake about a bit, and finally . . .

Emerge at 13. Sorry.

She stares at you for a moment, then sniffs. "Can't say I'm impressed by that," she says. "Not impressed at all. Are you impressed, Harold?"

The Cat shakes his head. "Singularly unimpressed," he says.

You wait for a moment, then ask, "Does this mean you're not going to tell me how to get to the Wizards' Guild?"

She sniffs again. "That's exactly what it means. I'd suggest you do a little revision of your Wizardry lessons before you come back here again. Meanwhile, Harold and I believe you should return to 48 and seek another destination since there is nothing for you here."

You heard the lady. Off you go to Section 48.

Section 131

"Tell you what—I'll come with you," says the little Apothecary cheerfully. "I might be of assistance to you in the ordeals and questions. Always like to give a young trainee a helping hand." He pops into the passageway and presses a button that closes the secret door behind you while switching on concealed lighting all along the passage. "Astral light, you'll notice," he comments. "Just go straight ahead. Quickly now."

You walk straight ahead as instructed, but before you can take more than half a dozen steps, a vast, archangelic form materializes directly in front of you. "Halt!" it commands. "My advice to you is to go back. But if you refuse, before you can proceed further you must answer me this: Which planet rules the Sun Sign Sagittarius?"

Another Wizardly riddle! You'd think they'd get tired of asking stuff like that by now. Still, let's look at your options. If you think it's the Sun, go to 14. For the Moon, go to 22. For Mercury, go to 30. For Venus, go to 45. For Mars, go to 59. For Jupiter, go to 68. For Saturn, go to 86. And, of course, if you haven't an idea, you can always take the Archangel's advice and make your way back to 48 where you can pick a less difficult destination. Or, indeed, fight your way past the Archangel at 115.

"Now this is our treasury, which you can loot if you like," says the Chief Troll as he conducts you on your tour. "And over there is an armory where you can equip yourself for any fights you may have in the future. Down there is an underpass that will take you off the island. That pathway leads you to the Wizards' Guild. But stay well clear of that tunnel—you shouldn't go in there under any circumstances whatsoever."

Ever get the feeling something's too good to be true? You can loot their treasury at 57, equip yourself at their armory at 76, take the underpass at 97, follow the path he says leads to the Wizards' Guild at 106, or explore the tunnel you shouldn't go into under any circumstances whatsoever at 151.

Section 133

There's something in here. You can't see it in the darkness, but you can hear it and you can certainly smell it. A sort of hot, sulphurous smell.

And apparently it can smell you, too, because it's just released a fireball that streaks toward you out of the darkness.

You could have done without that. Roll one die and subtract the score from your Life Points as the fireball strikes you. Then, as if you hadn't enough troubles, prepare yourself for a fight. It's only a little dragon hiding in the tunnel, but it does have 15 Life Points. If you lose the fight, go to 13. If not, you can clamber over the dragon's corpse and follow the tunnel all the way back to 1.

Section 134

You sit up with a jerk and look around you. To your absolute astonishment, the Wizards' Guild has disappeared, as has the mournful Wizard and, indeed, the entire island.

Leaving you standing gormlessly at 48.

Section 135

You twist and turn, turn and twist, return and retwist, coil, wriggle, back up, get confused, unconfuse yourself, snake about a bit, and finally . . .

Emerge at 48. Sorry.

How crass! How uncivilized! How revolting! It's a bear pit! They used to have these things all over the place in the days when people thought it entertaining to make animals fight each other for sport.

Fortunately there are no bears here at the moment, but there is a Guard as big as one. He lumbers over to you.

"You here for the fights?" he asks, jerking his thumb toward a notice advertising the next bear-baiting. "Bit early yet."

Here's a moral dilemma and no mistake. There's absolutely nothing to stop your walking away right now and picking another destination at 48. But do you honestly want to have it on your conscience that you did nothing to stop bear-baiting? If you're prepared to use it I can give you a one-time-only anti-bear-baiting spell so powerful it will close down this ghastly pit forever and make the villagers forget they ever thought it entertaining. The only thing is, you'll have to fight the Guard in order to use it, which means you could be killed and back to the beginning of your Wizard's Adventure. Even if you win, there's a chance the spell itself will kill you (some spells are like that). And none of this, absolutely none of it, gets you one inch nearer the Wizards' Guild. Rough choice. If you want the spell, the fight, and the danger, go to 144. But believe me, nobody will blame you if you walk away from this one.

Section 137

Bravely you hurl yourself upon him, dice rattling. Valiantly you throw sixes all over the place. Cunningly you cheat by quadrupling your Life Points.

The creature looks at you with absolute disdain. As he fangs you in the throat he murmurs:

> *What a silly thing to do*
> *And now you're landed in the stew*
> *For with the truth these words must ring*
> *You simply can't kill a dead thing!*

With the lines of this ghastly verse still ringing in your ears, you sink delicately to 13.

Section 138

You turn to retrace your steps and almost walk smack into a peculiar-looking individual in Wizard robes.

"Not the right place," he tells you mournfully.

"Pardon?"

"Not the place you want to go," he says. "Not the Wizards' Guild. It's an illusion. The Chief Troll hypnotized you—that's a bit of Advanced Wizardry you haven't learned about yet. The place you're looking for isn't even on this island."

You stare at him in bewilderment, wondering how you can know he's telling the truth.

"How do I know you're telling the truth?" you ask quickly.

The mournful Wizard sniffs. "Well, you can try moving toward it or backing away from it and see if it behaves like an illusion. Or, if you've already done that, you could ask me politely to break your hypnotic trance so you can see things the way they really are."

You can run at it again, at 65. Or move toward it more slowly at 89. Or back away at 119. But if none of that appeals, you can go to 103 and ask this mournful character to break the hypnotic trance he claims you're in. Except it doesn't feel like you're in an hypnotic trance, so you might just grab him by the throat and threaten dire things if he doesn't just come clean and use his Wizardly powers to let you reach the Guild building you can plainly see over there—all of which you can do at 142.

Section 139

"For a minute there I didn't think we were going to make it," says the Apothecary. "But I should have known your trusty pendulum wouldn't let you down."

You are back in the open air, somewhere outside the village. Behind you, the opening to the maze leads into a cliff face. Ahead of you, a short pathway leads to the shore of a still, dark lake.

"Where's the Wizards' Guild?" you ask.

"On an island in the lake," says the Apothecary promptly. "Your final little ordeal is to figure out how to get there."

"What about you?"

"Oh, I plan to fly on my broomstick, but I'm afraid it's only a single-seater so I can't give you a lift."

Quietly cursing the fact that *The Book of Wizardry* never taught you how to fly a broomstick, you walk to the lake shore. Beside a small jetty, a tall, thin, hooded boatman waits beside a notice announcing "C. H. Aron's Ferry." Beyond him, a fat man is offering free scuba gear tryouts, while further on a signpost proclaiming "Wizards' Guild" points to a newly constructed road tunnel that plunges underneath the lake. Beside it is a helicopter pad surrounded by notices proclaiming "Free Flights to the Island Every 15 Minutes."

*Spoilt for choice here. As the Apothecary takes flight on his single-seater broomstick, you can climb aboard the ferry at **165**, swim using the scuba gear at **146**, take the tunnel at **108**, or board a chopper at **78**.*

Section 140

Thankfully you emerge from the eerie, silent valley with its immortal guardian to discover that the path now widens into a real road. You follow the road for nearly three hours until, tired and hungry, you top a rise and see some distance ahead a picturesque village fortified by a wooden stockade wall. Since it seems unlikely you're going to find the Wizards' Guild today, this looks a reasonable place to pass the night.

You start down the hill, hoping there may be a decent inn in the village—and hoping you have enough gold to pay for lodgings and a decent meal. In moments, you have reached the gate of the stockade which, while open, is nonetheless guarded by a slack-jawed yokel.

"Where might you think you're going?" asks this character, leaning on his pitchfork and chewing a length of straw.

"I might think I was going to the moon," you tell him in your best sarcastic manner, "but, in point of fact, what I actually think is that I'm going to enter this fine village wherein to partake of some excellent victuals before spending a comfortable night between clean sheets in your most exclusive lodgings."

"That'll be eight gold pieces," says the yokel, not at all impressed.

"For a meal and a room?" you ask him, appalled.

"No, just to get past me," says the dufus. "Meal and a room is extra."

Well, here's another pretty pickle to be sure. Are you going to give this clown eight gold pieces of your hard-earned money? Do you even have *eight gold pieces* to give him? And if you have, do you have enough left to buy a meal and lodgings in this venal village? You can pay him the cash, if you have it, at **60**. Otherwise I suppose it's a frustrating time again and you can try fighting your way past him at **104**. Alternatively, of course, you could try sneaking round the back and jumping over the stockade wall in a single bound, but you'll have to risk an **Absolutely Anything Roll** for that. If you try, fail and kill yourself (just reminding you of the rules) go to **13**. If you succeed, count yourself a jammy dodger and troll off to **48**.

He scratches his head thoughtfully. "Guild . . . Guild . . . Yes, I think I have something inside that could be of help to you. Came in the post the other day. Come in and I'll see if I can find it for you."

You can follow him to 70 to see what it was that came in the post. Or, as always, you can cut this short and return to 48 to select another destination.

Section 142

You grab him by the throat and threaten dire things if he doesn't just come clean and use his Wizardly powers to let you reach the Guild building you can plainly see over there.

The mournful Wizard sighs deeply. "Would you like me to transport you to the actual spot where you think you can see the illusion?" he asks.

"I would! I would! I would!" you scream abusively.

He waves his Wand mournfully and transports you to 13.

Section 143

The villagers frog-march you to a building marked "Jail," sling you in a cell, and throw away the key.

*Leaving you to starve to death at 13, which should teach you not to go around murdering people who are only trying to do their job. (Or anybody else for that matter.) Alternatively, you might try a jail-break to add to your other crimes. That will require an **Absolutely Anything Roll**. If you succeed, you can return in disguise to 48, select another destination, and hopefully behave yourself a bit better this time. If you fail, you're off to 13 anyway.*

Section 144

You find yourself staring at an open book that has miraculously appeared in your hands. Luminous writing writhes and sparkles across its parchment pages, then forms itself into a single word . . . "thundermold"!

"Thundermold?" you whisper, frowning.

At once there is a rather moldy clap of thunder and a blinding flash of light. The world spins, a howling whirlwind fills your ears, and you are lifted bodily and thrown into the bear pit itself. Shakily you pull yourself to your feet and look around. To your horror, the Guard is in the pit with you, still wearing his Guard's uniform, but magically transformed into a huge black bear. His eyes flash red as he hurls himself upon you.

How much trouble can you get yourself into with one simple spell? The Bear-Guard has a massive 33 Life Points, just three short of the absolute maximum possible. He also does an additional three points fang-and-claw damage on every roll he scores against you. Doesn't look as if you stand a prayer here, but there's one tiny piece of good news—you've been changed into a bear as well, which doubles your previous Life Points and gives you the same additional three points fang-and-claw damage. If this helps you win the fight, you can find out what happens next at 29. If not, you can lick your wounds (a filthy habit) at 13.

Section 145

"Ready? Good. Now, the admission question for the Wizards' Guild is this: What color is the handle of a Wizard's Wing? Is it blue? Is it yellow? Is it red? Is it olive, citrine, russet, and black?"

Don't have to be the Brain of Boston to answer that one, do you? If you think it's blue, go to 25. For yellow, go to 39. If you'd prefer red, go to 56. Or give the olive, citrine, etc., answer at 71.

Section 146

The scuba gear doesn't fit all that well and the air hose appears to be Welsh since it has a small leak in it, but you put it on anyway and plunge into the still waters of the lake.

*This is quite chancy, you know. Better try an **Absolutely Anything Roll** to see if you make it to the island. If you don't and the attempt kills you, go to 13. If you succeed, go to 28. If you fail in the attempt and can't try again, you can still climb aboard the ferry at 165, take the tunnel at 108, or board a chopper at 78.*

Section 147

Three hundred yards along the road you walk into a poacher's snare and are caught fast by one leg (the right one.) You are still trying to free yourself when you are eaten by a bear. It starts by chewing off your foot (the left one) then munching through the side of your head, then eating—

*But you don't really want the details, do you? Go to **13**. And next time you might think of checking the Pyramid Oracle more carefully.*

Section 148

Cautiously you insert the golden key into the keyhole. It turns easily with a pronounced *click*. As you step back, there is a sinister creaking sound and the lid of the sarcophagus begins slowly to open. As it does so, a long, slim, white-gloved hand emerges from the coffin and grips the side as a deathly pale figure in evening dress and opera cloak slowly climbs out. He turns huge red eyes toward you, then slowly smiles, revealing long, pointed Dracula teeth. He takes a long, deep breath, then says:

> *Welcome to this lonely crypt*
> *Into which you now to have slipped.*
> *You've almost reached your destination*
> *Something which should give pleasure*
> *And joy to the entire nation.*

At once your blood runs cold. Only the black books of the most sinister Wizardry ever refer to this creature, yet from his appearance and speech, you have no doubt whatsoever about his identity. This can only be the notorious Poetic Fiend, renowned for his ability to produce the worst verse in the known universe.

*Yes, but what are you going to do about him? An **Absolutely Anything Roll** might allow you to run all the way back to 48 where you might find a less dangerous destination. But aside from that I suppose you could always take your chances with a surprise attack* on the Fiend at 137, although I have to tell you very few have tackled this character and lived to tell the tale. Your other possibility is to try to open up a dialogue with him at 67, although I have to tell you very few have done this and lived to tell the tale either. Sorry. It's been such a nice adventure so far.

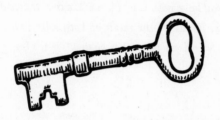

Section 149

"Auction!" calls the Apothecary, who has obviously been through this before.

The Trolls murmur in anticipation and fumble with their purses.

The way this works is straightforward. First, make a note of how much gold you have with you. Then make two double-dice rolls on behalf of the Trolls. If the result of both rolls added together is more than the gold you have, then go to 47. If it's less, go to 80.

Looks as if you've lucked out here! This is the village inn—and a pleasant enough looking place it is. You walk through the door to find a rosy-cheeked Landlord serving ale to a group of pie-eyed villagers who certainly should not be drinking at this hour of the day.

"Prithee, Landlord," you call out, getting into the spirit of the adventure, "dost thou have a meal and a warm bed for this weary traveller?"

"It's one gold for a meal, two for a bed. Dost this weary traveller have any dosh?" the Landlord asks you cynically.

Good question. If you have three gold pieces, you can have a meal and a bed at 12. If you have only two, you can have a meal at 32 or a bed at 61, but not both. If you have only one, you can have a meal at 32 but not a bed. If you have none, you can have a word with the Landlord at 91. If you're fed up with all this crass commercialism, you can go back to 48 and select another destination.

Section 151

Gaily you skip along the tunnel. Happily you ignore the distant rumbling sound. Merrily you are buried under 78,000 tons of rock as the whole thing caves in.

Should have listened to the Troll. Go to 13.

With the stupid lion knocking you off balance by rubbing its head against your leg, you cautiously explore the stone-flagged chamber. Apart from the passage through which you entered, there is a stairway leading upwards to a set of locked iron gates. In the chamber itself, you discover the sarcophagus is also locked, which is maybe as well since there's a brass plaque screwed into one side announcing:

Crypt of the Fiend
(Open only with a Golden Key)

If you happen to have a golden key, you can open the sarcophagus at 161. If you don't, your only option is to backtrack carefully the way you came and select another destination at 48.

Section 153

"Eeeaaaaaagh!" you scream, running round the island like a headless chicken.

*Getting out of this mess requires an **Absolutely Anything Roll.** If the roll kills you, go to 13. If it succeeds, go to 40. If it fails without killing you, you can still fight him at 99, or follow him quietly at 124.*

The path gets narrower and narrower. The sky gets darker and darker. The surroundings get silenter and silenter. It starts to rain. Poisonous fumes erupt from volcanic cracks. You turn a corner and walk right into a crouching Sphinx.

(I told you! I warned you! But did you listen? Of course not. Sphinxes are immortal—can't be killed no matter how many dice you roll. Immortal and lethal if you get on the wrong side of them. Oh, well, too late now. You've made your bed and now you'll just have to lie on it.)

"Hi, Oedipus," says the Sphinx.

"I'm not Oedipus," you tell her.

"Big mistake," says the Sphinx. "Old 'Puss was the only one who ever got the answer to my riddle. And you know what happens to anybody who doesn't get the answer to my riddle?"

You swallow. "No."

"I beat them to a pulp," says the Sphinx smugly. "Then I tear them to pieces. Then I decapitate them. Then I jump up and down on any bits that are left. Then I—"

"Okay, okay, I get the idea!" you cut her short. "This riddle of yours—it wouldn't be the one about what walks on four legs, then two, then three would it?"

"Don't be naive," says the Sphinx scornfully. "Everybody knows that one now. Dear me, no. I've quite a different riddle now and you have to answer it correctly, otherwise I'll beat you to a pulp, tear you to pieces, decapitate you, jump up and—"

"All right, already! I get the idea. Just ask me the riddle!" you scream.

The Sphinx smiles mysteriously and says, "The riddle of the Sphinx is this: Which Magical Square adds up to 65?"

Bad luck! That's about as difficult a riddle as a Wizard could be asked. Still, you've a one-in-seven chance of guessing it if you don't actually know. If you think the answer is the Square of the Sun, turn to 111. If you think it might be the Square of the Moon, go to 18. For the Square of Mercury, try 8. If you think it's the Square of Venus, go to 4. If the Square of Mars appeals to you, turn to 88. If you think it might be the Square of Saturn, try 15. And good luck.

You twist and turn, turn and twist, return and retwist, coil, wriggle, back up, get confused, unconfuse yourself, snake about a bit, and finally . . .

Emerge at 48. Sorry.

Section 156

"Honestly?" He blinks. "Will you really? I mean, do you cross your heart and hope to die?"

"Of course," you nod reassuringly. "Integrity is my middle name."

At which this lunatic waves goodbye to the Trolls and conducts you back to 48 where you're free to select another destination. Don't forget to send him the money, heh-heh.

Section 157

What a very strange place. First of all, the smell hits you like a trip-hammer as you open the door. Next of all, it's gloomy to the point of darkness, even though it's obviously a shop.

You stand inside the entrance listening to the fading echoes of the jingly doorbell and wait for your eyes to grow accustomed to the gloom. When they do so, the shop gets stranger still. Shelves are full of the oddest mixtures—pickled bits of animals, boxes of dried herbs, powdered minerals. One section is prominently marked POISONS. There are things labeled DRAGON CLAWS and WYVERN WINGS. There are several stuffed crocodiles hanging from the ceiling.

A little man in rimless spectacles emerges from a back room to peer at you short-sightedly in a Welsh accent. "A Trainee Wizard, look you. Looking for the Wizards' Guild, isn't it?"

"Well, yes, it is," you tell him, somewhat taken aback by his turn of phrase.

"In that case you've come to the right place. The exact right place. My humble apothecary shop is actually a hidden portal to the Wizards' Guild. Never think it, would you? If you can give me the right answer to a simple question, you can join at once. Are you ready to answer the question now?"

Is the Pope a Catholic? Of course you're ready to answer the question now! You are, aren't you? I mean, if you aren't, you can always return to 48 and pick another destination. But if you are, run down to 145 where you can pass the final exam.

Section 158

Three minutes after you take off, the Pilot reports engine trouble. Two minutes after that, the rotor blades catch fire. Following which the fuel tank explodes, the Pilot bails out and the whole machine turns into a fireball that plunges into the waters below.

No wonder you were feeling blue. Climb out of the wreckage on the lakebed and quietly drown at 13.

Section 159

You spend the night tossing and turning on the straw and get up the following morning pitted with flea bites. Since bed doesn't include breakfast, you drag yourself hungrily from the inn, muttering something about never staying there again.

Yes, well, this is what you get if you let yourself be pushed around in the Wizard's Adventure. Off you go to 48 now and see if you can find yourself a more appealing destination.

Section 160

You squeeze into the crev—you squeeze into the—you try to squeeze into—you get stuck while trying to squeeze into the crevice.

Too many donuts, I'm afraid. But what are you going to do now? Better roll two dice. Score 2 to 6 and you manage to pop through after a struggle with no harm done. Score 7 to 12 and you manage to pop through after a struggle leaving a bit of skin and two Life Points behind. Either way, you've squeezed into 5.

Cautiously you insert the golden key into the keyhole. It turns easily with a pronounced *click*. As you step back, there is a sinister creaking sound and the lid of the sarcophagus begins slowly to open. As it does so, a long, slim, white-gloved hand emerges from the coffin and grips the side as a deathly pale figure in evening dress and opera cloak slowly climbs out. He turns huge red eyes toward you then slowly smiles, revealing long, pointed Dracula teeth. He takes a long, deep breath, then says:

> *Welcome to this lonely crypt*
> *Into which you now to have slipped.*
> *You've almost reached your destination*
> *Something which should give pleasure*
> *And joy to the entire nation.*

At once your blood runs cold. Only the black books of the most sinister Wizardry ever refer to this creature, yet from his appearance and speech, you have no doubt whatsoever about his identity. This can only be the notorious Poetic Fiend, renowned for his ability to produce the worst verse in the known universe.

*Yes, but what are you going to do about him? An **Absolutely Anything Roll** might allow you to run all the way back to 48 where you might find a less dangerous destination. But aside from that I suppose you could always take your chances with a surprise attack* on the Fiend at **137**, although I have to tell you very few have tackled this character and lived to tell the tale. Your other possibility is to try to open up a dialogue with him at **101**, although I have to tell you very few have done this and lived to tell the tale either. Sorry. It's been such a nice adventure so far.

Section 162

"Witch, Wizard, and Blacksmith," mutters the Well Monster incomprehensibly as you deliver the fatal blow. Then it adds sinisterly, as it begins to sink beneath the murky waters, "I'll be back!"

But the return of the Well Monster is the least of your worries since you're beginning to sink beneath the murky waters as well.

*This requires an **Absolutely Anything Roll**, the only way to find out whether you're able to climb out of the well in your weakened state. If you win the roll, you can make your way back to 48 to find another destination. If not, I'm afraid you can only ponder what the Monster meant about Witch, Wizard, and Blacksmith at 13. Good luck.*

Section 163

"Nope, still don't know," he tells you, pocketing your money with a big grin.

*That's really irritating. You can try to beat it out of him at **125**. Or stop wasting time with this clown and go to **48** where you can pick another destination.*

Section 164

Grimly you explore every inch of the ruin. Just as you are about to give up in disgust, you suddenly find—

Nothing. Absolutely nothing. That hollow laugh must have been your imagination. Get yourself back to 48 and see if you can find a more fruitful destination.

Section 165

You climb into the back of the boat and settle yourself comfortably as the ferryman casts off. The boat glides silently out onto the still, dark waters.

As it does so, the boatman's hood falls back to reveal a skull beneath.

Surprised you fell for that one. "C. H. Aron" indeed. That's Charon, you idiot! Ferryman of the dead in ancient mythology. And now ferrying you direct to 13.

Section 166

She stares at you for a moment, then sniffs. "Can't say I'm impressed by that," she says. "Not impressed at all. Are you impressed, Harold?"

The Cat shakes his head. "Singularly unimpressed," he says.

You wait for a moment, then ask, "Does this mean you're not going to tell me how to get to the Wizards' Guild?"

She sniffs again. "That's exactly what it means. I'd suggest you do a little revision of your Wizardry lessons before you come back here again. Meanwhile, Harold and I believe you should return to 48 and seek another destination since there is nothing for you here."

You heard the lady. Off you go to Section 48.

Section 167

Heart pounding from the fight, you step over the body of the lion and cautiously explore the stone-flagged chamber. Apart from the passage through which you entered, there is a stairway leading upwards to a set of locked iron gates. In the chamber itself, you discover the sarcophagus is also locked, which is just as well since there's a brass plaque screwed into one side announcing:

Crypt of the Fiend
(Open only with a Golden Key)

If you happen to have a golden key, you can open the sarcophagus at 148. If you don't, your only option is to backtrack carefully the way you came and select another destination at 48.

He stares at you with a pained expression. "This is devastating," he says. "I really thought you were home and dry. That's the *wrong* answer! I can't believe it. You've come so far. Just this one final hurdle and suddenly you're goosed. Done for. Relegated to the ranks of the terminally ordinary. Why on earth didn't you sneakily look up the answer before you gave it? It's there in the lesson about Wizard Space. I can't let you come this far and dump you right back at the beginning. Tell you what: You do a bit of revision on the Wizard Space lesson and you can restart your adventure with all your Life Points, golden keys, and other stuff absolutely intact at 48. Just work your way from there and get it right next time!"

You heard what the man said. Go to Wizard Space, then 48.

Section 169

You twist and turn, turn and twist, return and retwist, coil, wriggle, back up, get confused, unconfuse yourself, snake about a bit, and finally . . .

Emerge at 48. Sorry.

"How kind! How civilized! How sweet!" you trill innocently. "How delighted I am to accept your generous hospitality, for it is some time since I have eaten so that even the contents of your smelly pot seem appetizing. Perhaps I might ask you to lead the way into your charming home so that we may partake of the feast you have offered."

The wizened old Crone, who seems to have grown a hump on her back since the last time you saw her, scratches her hooked nose and cackles, "Walk this way, young person, walk this way. I haven't lunched on—with, I mean *with*—a tender young person in several months."

So saying, she rises and hobbles into her grimy old cottage, glancing over her shoulder encouragingly.

Look, are you really sure you want to do this? You've read the fairy tales as much as I have—that old cow is obviously a Witch and the chances are you're going to end up as an ingredient in her next smelly potion. Why not just turn around and get yourself back to 48 where you can pick a nice safe different destination. But since it's your adventure, you're perfectly entitled to follow her into the grimy old cottage at 107.

Appendix:
The Theban Alphabet
of Honorious

The old Wizards of days gone by were fascinated by strange alphabets. None was stranger than the so-called Theban Alphabet of Honorius. Honorius III was not just a Wizard but a pope (from 1216 to 1227). He was reputed to keep a spirit locked up in a ring he wore and made the Vatican Palace shake when he spoke to it. I don't know if it was this spirit who gave him the Theban Alphabet, but he got hold of it somewhere. This is what it looked like:

a   b   c   d   e

f   g   h   i   k

l   m   n   o   p

q   r   s   t   v

x   y   z